Family
Secrets

Christy® Fiction Series

Christy® Fiction Series

Family
Secrets

Catherine Marshall

adapted by C. Archer

WORD PUBLISHING
Dallas·London·Vancouver·Melbourne

FAMILY SECRETS
Book Eight in the *Christy*® Fiction Series

Managing Editor: Laura Minchew
Project Editor: Beverly Phillips

Library of Congress Cataloging-in-Publication Data

Archer, C. 1956–
   Family secrets / Catherine Marshall ; adapted by C. Archer.
      p.   cm. — (Christy fiction series ; 8)
   "Word kids!"
   Summary: Many residents of Cutter Gap are upset when a black
family moves in, but Christy steps in to help when a series of
threatening incidents befalls the new neighbors.
   ISBN 0–8499–3959–3 (pbk.)
   [1. Prejudices—Fiction. 2. Afro-Americans—Fiction. 3. Teachers—
Fiction. 4. Mountain life—Fiction. 5. Christian life—Fiction.]
   I. Marshall, Catherine, 1914–1983. Christy. II. Title.
   III. Series : Archer, C., 1956– Christy fiction series ; 8.
PZ7.A6725Fam   1996
[Fic]—dc20

                                                              96–30503
                                                                   CIP
                                                                    AC

Printed in the United States of America

96 97 98 99 00 OPM 9 8 7 6 5 4 3 2 1

The Characters

CHRISTY RUDD HUDDLESTON, a nineteen-year-old girl.

CHRISTY'S STUDENTS:
ROB ALLEN, age fourteen.
FESTUS ALLEN, age twelve.
CREED ALLEN, age nine.
DELLA MAY ALLEN, age eight.
LITTLE BURL ALLEN, age six.
WANDA BECK, age eight.
WRAIGHT HOLT, age seventeen.
VELLA HOLT, age five.
MOUNTIE O'TEALE, age ten.
MARY O'TEALE, age eight.
RUBY MAE MORRISON, age thirteen.
CLARA SPENCER, age twelve.
ZADY SPENCER, age ten.
LUNDY TAYLOR, age seventeen.
LOUISE WASHINGTON, age fifteen.
JOHN WASHINGTON, age ten.
HANNAH WASHINGTON, age eight.

DOCTOR NEIL MACNEILL, the physician of the Cove.
HELEN MACNEILL, the doctor's grandmother.

ALICE HENDERSON, a Quaker missionary who started the mission at Cutter Gap.

DAVID GRANTLAND, the young minister.
IDA GRANTLAND, David's sister and the mission housekeeper.

JAMES BRILEY, former classmate of Doctor MacNeill.

BOB ALLEN, keeper of the mill by Blackberry Creek.
MARY ALLEN, Bob's wife.
   *(Parents of Christy's students Rob, Festus,
   Creed, Della May, and Little Burl.)*
GRANNY ALLEN, Bob's grandmother.

CURTIS WASHINGTON, new arrival to Cutter Gap
   from Virginia.
MARGARET WASHINGTON, Curtis's wife.
   *(Parents of Christy's students Louise, John,
   and Hannah, and of Etta, a baby girl.)*
WILLIAM WASHINGTON, Curtis's grandfather, an
   escaped slave.

LANCE BARCLAY, an old beau of Christy's from
   Asheville.

GRANNY O'TEALE, a mountain woman.
SWANNIE O'TEALE, Granny's daughter-in-law.
   (Mother of Christy's students Mountie and Mary.)

AUNT POLLY TEAGUE, the oldest woman in the Cove

FAIRLIGHT SPENCER, Christy's closest friend in the Cove.
   (Mother of Christy's students Clara and Zady.)

LETTY COBURN, a mountain woman.

SCALAWAG, Creed Allen's pet raccoon.
VIOLET, a pet mouse belonging to Hannah
   Washington.
PRINCE, a black stallion donated to the mission.

❧ One ❧

This is without a doubt the messiest cabin I have ever seen!" Christy Huddleston exclaimed.

Doctor Neil MacNeill gave a hearty laugh. "I'm a doctor, Christy, not a housekeeper."

"Look at this dust." Christy wrote her name in the thick dust layering a cupboard full of medical books. "It's a good thing you don't perform surgery in this room."

"Actually, I do, on occasion."

Christy pointed to a stuffed deer head mounted on the wall. "Those antlers are covered with spider webs, Neil!"

Doctor MacNeill crossed his arms over his chest, hazel eyes sparkling. "I was under the impression you were sent here by Miss Alice to pick up some medical supplies. If I'd known there was going to be a housekeeping inspection, I would have prepared." Playfully, he tossed a feather duster at Christy. "Since you're so concerned, please feel free to take a whack at the dust."

"I can't stay *that* long. Besides, anyone who can perform delicate surgery can surely figure out how to operate a feather duster," Christy replied, laughing. "Before heading back to the mission, I thought I'd say hello to your new neighbors. How are the Washingtons doing, anyway?"

"Just getting settled in." The doctor began filling a small glass bottle with the dark, bitter-smelling medicine he and Miss Alice used to treat whooping cough. "They're in that abandoned cabin, but it's going to need a lot of repairs. Nice family. Four kids, three school-age."

"That'll bring my grand total up to seventy students," Christy said. "Amazing. When I decided to come here to Cutter Gap to teach, I pictured perhaps twenty children in my schoolroom at the most. But seventy! That's quite a handful."

The doctor grinned. He was a big man, with rugged, handsome features that looked like they'd been chiseled out of rough stone. His curly, sandy-red hair, always in need of a comb, gave him a boyish look. "For most mere mortals, that many students would be impossible," he said. "But for you, my dear Miss Huddleston, nothing is impossible."

Christy reached for the next empty new bottle and held it steady while the doctor filled it with medicine. His hands were rough and stained, the mark of long years caring for the desperately poor residents of this Tennessee mountain cove. Although Christy had lived here several months, her own hands seemed fragile and soft by comparison. They were the hands of a "city-gal," as the mountain people would say.

In some ways she still was that fresh-faced girl from Asheville, North Carolina—frightened, but full of big dreams. Her wide blue eyes and delicate features made her look younger than her nineteen years. She wore her sun-streaked hair swept up to make herself look older, but Christy knew it didn't fool anyone.

The doctor put a stopper in each of the two bottles he'd just filled. He gazed around the cabin with a critical eye. "Maybe you're right," he said. "This place could use a good cleaning."

It was a simple cabin, but well-furnished by mountain standards. A bearskin rug lay on the hearth. An old cherry clock ticked on the mantel. A rack of antlers served as a coat rack. A hunting rifle was propped against the wall in the corner, and a pipe with an engraved silver band rested in the pipe rack by a chair. Framed, inscribed photos, most from the doctor's years at medical school, peered out from the dusty shelves.

"Christy," the doctor said, "there's something I've been meaning to tell you. Um, ask you. It's about—" he cleared his throat, "well, about a wedding, actually."

Christy blinked in surprise. "A wedding?"

"Yes, that's right. And a confession I have to make."

The doctor's fingers were trembling as he reached for another empty bottle. It wasn't like him to be so nervous, and it certainly wasn't like him to blush!

Christy gulped. She'd already been through one proposal since coming to Cutter Gap. David Grantland, the mission's young minister, had asked for her hand in marriage not long ago. In the end, despite her affection for David, Christy had told him no. She'd explained that she needed more time to be sure of her feelings. She cared for David. But she also cared deeply for Doctor MacNeill— perhaps more than she was willing to admit, even to herself.

"What do you mean, 'confession'?" Christy asked, not sure she was ready to hear the answer. "What are you trying to say, Neil?"

He took a deep breath. "Is it hot in here?"

"Not really."

The doctor fanned his face with his hand.

"It's definitely hot. Why don't we go out on the porch?"

They settled into the old oak rockers on the cabin porch. Tulip trees and giant beeches formed a graceful canopy, shading out most of the hot late afternoon sun. "It's so beautiful here," Christy said, thinking it might be a good idea to change the subject.

"Yes, it is," the doctor replied. "I was born in this cabin, did you know that? So was my grandfather, and his grandfather before him. Sometimes I think these mountains are in my blood." He looked over at Christy, a pained expression on his face. "A man could do much worse. Couldn't he?"

"Neil," Christy said gently, "what is it you're trying to tell me?"

He rubbed his eyes. "It's silly, really. Crazy, even."

"Tell me."

"Well, it's like this." He took a deep breath. "I have an old friend by the name of James Briley. We went to medical school together. We were roommates, best friends—and competitors, I suppose. James went on to establish a thriving practice in Knoxville. He invited me to join him, and I was sorely tempted. But I felt an obligation to come back to Cutter Gap and help the people here. There wasn't a doctor within a hundred miles of this place. This was where I was needed."

"You did the right thing, Neil."

"I suppose." The doctor shrugged. "The thing is, it seems James is getting married, and he's invited me to the wedding."

"Oh!" Christy exclaimed. "So *that's* what you meant!"

"What did you think I meant?"

"I thought . . ." It was Christy's turn to blush. "I mean, I know it's crazy, but I thought you—"

"You thought I was going to propose to you?" The doctor threw back his head and laughed.

"Well, it isn't *that* funny," Christy protested.

"Isn't one proposal a year enough for you?" Doctor MacNeill asked, still chuckling.

"You can stop laughing now."

"I'm sorry. You'll understand why it's so funny when I explain my predicament. It's really quite amusing, actually. You see, James's letters are always full of automobiles and exotic trips and his beautiful house and his famous patients. My letters—well, let's just say a successful possum hunt can't quite measure up. I know I shouldn't feel that way, but it's hard . . ."

"No, you shouldn't. You have a wonderful life here in Cutter Gap."

"Seems it's even better now. A few letters

ago, when I learned James was engaged, I sort of let it slip that I'd become engaged myself." The doctor forced a laugh. "You'll get a good laugh out of this when I tell you . . ."

Christy tapped her foot on the wooden porch. "Try me."

"Well," the doctor said uncomfortably, "I sort of casually mentioned to old James that you and I were sort of . . ."

"Yes?"

"Sort of engaged."

⚜ TWO ⚜

Y ou *what?"* Christy cried.

"I know, I know." The doctor held up his hands. "I can't believe I did it, either. But if you knew James, Christy, you'd understand. We were rivals over everything. We always came in first and second on exams. One week it would be James, the next week, me. We were even rivals for the same girls."

"Oh?" Christy asked with a cool smile. "And who usually won that little competition?"

The doctor jumped from his chair and began pacing the length of the wooden porch. "I don't blame you for being annoyed. It was stupid. Not like me at all, actually." He paused. "I love Cutter Gap. I chose to be here. I didn't want the fancy practice and the other fancy things."

"Just the fancy wife," Christy said.

He rolled his eyes. "It's not like that, Christy. I was just . . . spinning a little fantasy on paper. I was going through a dark time awhile back. I was having some doubts about my choice to stay here. David had just proposed to you, and maybe that put the idea in my head. I don't know. Obviously, I never thought it would come to anything."

"And now it has?"

The doctor pulled an envelope from the pocket of his plaid hunting shirt. "Yes, in the form of that wedding invitation. James insists on meeting you. He can't wait to see you dance with the waltz champion of Tennessee."

"And that would be—"

"Uh, me." Doctor MacNeill gave a sheepish grin. "What can I say? I exaggerated a little."

"Is there anything else you exaggerated about?"

"Well, your father is a wealthy industrialist. Very well-off. And you speak four languages."

"Only four?"

"I didn't want to get carried away."

Christy stared at the doctor in disbelief. This was so unlike the down-to-earth, practical Neil MacNeill she knew! She was torn between teasing him, yelling at him, and feeling sorry for him.

"I also told James," he continued, "that you were the most beautiful girl I'd ever set eyes on. Not to mention the toughest and smartest."

"More lies . . ."

"No," the doctor said softly. "All that was the truth."

Christy felt her cheeks burn.

"Well, I appreciate your telling me this, Neil. As long as you tell James the truth, I suppose there's no harm done."

"That's the thing, Christy," the doctor said, then hesitated. "I was thinking maybe we could go."

"*Go?* And pretend to be engaged and all the rest?"

"What could it hurt?"

"Well, I can think of a few little problems with your plan. First, I speak one language, not four. Second, my father is not a wealthy industrialist. Third, I'm not much of a dancer—even if you *are*. And—oh yes. There's that little matter of our imaginary engagement." Christy folded her arms over her chest. "Besides, it would be lying, Neil. And that would be wrong."

"You wouldn't have to lie." The doctor winked. "I'll present you as Miss Christy Rudd Huddleston of Asheville, North Carolina."

"Neil, you know very well that James will presume the rest. What if he speaks to me in Italian while we're waltzing?"

"You just bat your eyes and smile. I'll say you're very shy. Besides, your dance card will be full." The doctor took her hand and gave an awkward bow. "You'll be dancing with me all night. After all, whom do you think I won my imaginary waltz championship with, anyway?"

"Let me guess—your imaginary fiancée?"

"How'd you guess? Actually, I did win a local dance contest a few years back. So I've only partially stretched the truth."

Before she could object, the doctor pulled Christy from her chair and swept her into his arms. "May I have this dance, Miss Huddleston?"

"Neil," Christy said, groaning, "I am not going to go along with your plan—"

"Just one dance."

She allowed herself a small smile. "Well, all right. I mean, *oui, monsieur.* Which, incidentally, is the sum total of the French I know."

Humming an old mountain tune, Doctor MacNeill swept Christy around the porch in dizzying circles. "That's not exactly a waltz, you know," she chided.

"I know. But I'm better at this."

"How is it you managed to win that imaginary championship, I wonder?" Christy teased.

"The judges were swept away by my partner's beauty," the doctor replied.

"Neil," Christy said as they whirled, "you have to tell James the truth, you know."

As suddenly as he'd swept her into his arms, the doctor let go of Christy. He went to the porch railing, staring out at the deep green woods.

"Tell James the truth? Tell him that I have to beg for medical supplies from old classmates? Tell him that I perform surgery in the most primitive conditions imaginable? Tell him that I spend my days sewing up the wounds caused by ignorance and hate and feuding?"

Gently Christy touched his shoulder. "Neil, what's wrong? Why all this self-doubt all of a sudden?"

"I don't know. Maybe it started when I sold that parcel of land to the Washingtons. They're good people, and I was happy to give them the chance to make a home here. But when I signed over that deed, I started wondering what's kept me attached to this particular place so long."

"You were born here. You have roots here."

"You were born in North Carolina. And here you are, far from home, because you wanted to help change people's lives."

"You've changed people's lives right here, too."

"I wonder sometimes . . ." He sighed heavily. "I just wonder if my life has come to anything. If what I've done here matters."

"Of course it—" Christy stopped short. She pointed toward the woods.

Two small figures were approaching fast. "That's Creed Allen," Christy said, waving, "and Della May."

Creed, who was nine, was holding his pet raccoon Scalawag in his arms, wrapped in an old shirt. His eight-year-old sister followed close behind.

"What a surprise," Christy said. "What brings the two of you here?"

"Hey, Miz Christy," Creed said softly.

"Hey, Teacher," Della May said.

"Is Scalawag all right?" Christy asked.

"He's feelin' a mite poorly is all," Creed said. He glanced over his shoulder nervously.

"Well, I generally tend to humans, but if you bring Scalawag on in, I'll have a look at him," Doctor MacNeill said cheerfully.

There was a noise in the woods. Della May gulped. "We'd best be headin' inside," she whispered to Creed.

"Creed," Christy said, "is there something worrying you?"

But before the boy could respond, Christy realized the answer.

A man burst from the thick trees. He was dressed in a worn black coat and was wearing a battered hat. In his right hand was a shotgun. The man was Bob Allen, the children's father. He was the keeper of the mill by Blackberry Creek.

13

"What do you young'uns mean, comin' here?" Bob cried. "I done told you not to go near this place no more!"

Christy had never seen Bob Allen so out of control.

"But Scalawag's sick, Pa," Creed said. "I had to do something."

"Bob?" Doctor MacNeill asked. "What's wrong?"

Bob strode up to the porch steps. A scowl was fixed on his grizzled face. He looked Doctor MacNeill in the eye and spat on the ground.

"I'll tell you what's wrong. What's wrong is you sold your land to them what don't belong here. Cutter Gap's a place for white folks, and white folks only. Now, I was goin' huntin' for squirrel, but these bullets will work just as well on a low-down skunk like you."

Slowly, his hand trembling, Bob raised his shotgun and aimed it straight at Doctor MacNeill.

"Bob," Christy whispered in horror, "please don't—"

"What the doc done was plain wrong, Miz Christy," Bob muttered.

He cocked the gun. Christy jumped at the awful sound.

"And now," Bob said, "he's a-goin' to pay for it."

⊰ Three ⊱

N o, Pa, no!" Creed cried.

Della May yanked on her father's arm, but Bob brushed her aside. He jerked his gun at the doctor. "You got no right mixin' up the races thataway."

"The Washingtons paid me for that land, fair and square, Bob," the doctor said. "They have as much right to be here as you and I do."

"My family and yours, we've been neighbors long as memory serves. My granny and yours were friends, Doc. Now you've done gone and put them people in amongst us. It ain't fair and it ain't right, and it's a-goin' to cause more trouble than you ever saw in all your born days."

"It was my land to sell," the doctor said firmly. "The Washingtons came to me and made a fair offer, and I accepted it."

Again Bob spat on the ground. The hate in his eyes made Christy shiver. She glanced at Creed and Della May. They seemed frozen in place, as frightened by their father's wrath as she was.

"My kin ain't never had nothin' to do with their kind. Never have. Never will."

"What kind is that?" Christy asked pointedly.

"You blind, woman? Take a look at the color o' their skin!"

"If they're good neighbors, Bob," Christy said, "does it really matter if they're black or brown or blue or purple?"

"It matters. It matters something awful. You oughta see Granny Allen. She's got herself all into a tizzy about this. Can't eat, can't sleep a wink for fear o' what could happen. I'm here today to stand up for her rights. And for all my kin."

"Bob, I understand you're upset," Doctor MacNeill said. "Why don't you put down that gun and come on inside? If we talk about this—"

"Too late for talkin'." Bob paused, closing his eyes for a split second. When he opened them, he seemed confused. Then his gaze seemed to clear.

"Pa?" Creed whispered. "You all right?"

"I'll be right as rain when the doc here tells me he's a-goin' to kick them squatters off'n his land."

16

"They aren't squatters, Bob," Doctor MacNeill said. "They bought that land. It's theirs."

Slowly, Bob climbed the porch steps. He jabbed the end of his shotgun hard against the doctor's chest. "I can't let this happen," Bob said, almost pleading. "Your kin go back as far as mine, Doc. You got blood in this soil, same as me." He looked into the doctor's eyes, his face full of pain. "Don't make me do this. I don't want to shoot you."

Doctor MacNeill stood perfectly still, the picture of calm. Christy couldn't believe his composure. She was trembling like a leaf.

"You do what you have to do, Bob," the doctor said. "But the Washingtons are staying."

Bob took a deep breath. Again he closed his eyes, swaying slightly. Della May sobbed softly.

Christy watched Bob's finger on the trigger begin to move, slowly, slowly—

"No!" she cried. She locked her hand on the cold steel muzzle. "Doctor MacNeill saved your life, Bob. I was there that day he operated on you in the Spencers' cabin. You would have died without him, Bob. How can you do this?"

Bob's mouth moved, but he didn't speak. He slowly released the trigger. His eyelids dropped. His face went slack. Suddenly the shotgun slipped from his grasp. A moment later, Bob slumped to the porch.

"Pa!" Della May cried, rushing up the steps.

Doctor MacNeill knelt down. "He's passed out. Give me a hand, Christy. We'll take him into the cabin."

With his arms around Bob's chest, the doctor lifted him off the porch. Christy took Bob's feet. They carried him to the doctor's bedroom and placed him on the bed. Creed and Della May stood at the end of the bed, watching solemnly.

"He's been havin' these spells some lately," Creed said. "Ever since that tree done hit him on the head and you operated on him."

"Why didn't he come see me?" the doctor asked irritably as he reached for his medical bag.

"He was afeared he couldn't pay—" Della May began, but Creed sent her a warning look.

"Hush, Della May," he snapped.

Della May shot him a defiant look. "Teacher," she asked, "is Pa going to be okay?"

"If anyone can help your father, Doctor MacNeill can," Christy said.

She stroked the little girl's hair. Della May was a dainty, fairylike child, with shimmering red-blond hair. Like her brother, she had a sprinkling of freckles across the bridge of her nose. Creed, who had a mischievous streak, had always reminded Christy of Tom Sawyer. Della May was much quieter, but she had more than a little of her brother's stubbornness.

"He's coming to," the doctor said.

Bob's lids fluttered. He sat up on his elbows, frowning. "What in tarnation am I doin' here?"

"You passed out," Doctor MacNeill said, "and I gather this isn't the first time, either."

Bob shrugged. "I get my spells now and again. 'Tain't nothin'."

"It may be a result of your accident. Some lingering brain damage. If that's the case, I'm not sure there's much I can do for you, Bob. In a bigger city, with better facilities . . ."

Pushing the doctor aside, Bob climbed to his feet. "One thing and one thing only you can do for me. Get rid o' them Washingtons. If you don't do it, someone else will."

Doctor MacNeill locked his hand on Bob's shoulder. "Let me make one thing clear. Leave the Washingtons alone, or you'll have me to contend with. Understand?"

"Ain't just me who wants 'em gone. Everyone in Cutter Gap feels the same as I do."

"Not everyone," Christy said.

Bob looked at her with contempt. "You'll be sorry for this, the both of you. Come on, Creed, Della May."

Christy and the doctor followed the Allens onto the porch, where Bob retrieved his gun.

"Did you want me to take a look at Scalawag, Creed?" Doctor MacNeill asked.

"Creed!" Bob snapped. "Come on, boy!"

Creed stroked the raccoon's head. "He'll be

all right, I reckon, Doctor MacNeill. He's just goin' through a bad spell. It'll pass."

Christy watched Creed and Della May race after their father. "Just a bad spell," she repeated. "I wish we could say the same for Creed's father."

❧ Four ❧

Y ou really don't have to come with me,"
Christy said as she and the doctor made their
way along the path toward the Washingtons'
property a short time later. "I'm sure Bob
went straight home."

"Maybe," the doctor said darkly, "but you
can be equally sure that's not the end of
things. He's going to make trouble. And if he
doesn't, someone else will."

"The look on his face . . ." Christy shuddered. "Where do people learn that kind of
hate? These mountains are so beautiful, it's
hard to understand that kind of hate here."

Doctor MacNeill held back a low-hanging
oak branch so Christy could pass. "You've
been in these mountains long enough to
know the answer to that, Christy. They learn
it from their families and their friends. Look

21

at the feuds still burning in these hills. It's the same with prejudice like Bob's. It festers, like an old wound. Hate can grow in anyone's heart."

"Unless God is allowed to remove it," Christy added.

Up ahead, a sunny clearing came into view. In the center was a small, rundown cabin. The musical voices of children floated on the breeze. Two spotted hound dogs ran to greet Christy and the doctor, yelping happily.

"Pa!" a young girl in blue overalls cried. "Someone's comin'!"

A tall, thin man ran out from behind the house. In his hands was a shotgun.

"It's Neil MacNeill, Curtis!" the doctor called.

Instantly the man lowered his gun and broke into a smile. "Doctor! Thank goodness it's you. Good to see you again." He ran down the path and shook the doctor's hand.

"This is Miss Christy Huddleston, Curtis," Doctor MacNeill said. "She's the teacher over at the mission school."

"Please, you must excuse my manners, Miz Huddleston," Curtis apologized. "The gun, I mean. We're feelin' a little, well . . . nervous today."

"Problems?" the doctor asked.

"You tell me. Come on, I'll show you."

Curtis led them toward the house. "Children!" he called. "Come meet your new teacher. Margaret, we got ourselves some company!"

A pretty woman wearing a white apron emerged from the cabin. She smiled shyly.

"This is my wife, Margaret," Curtis said. "Margaret, you remember Doctor MacNeill. And this here's Miz Christy Huddleston, the mission teacher."

"It's an honor to have you visitin'," Margaret said. "I'm afraid we're just gettin' settled in. I wish I'd known you were comin'. I could have fixed up some o' my cornbread for you and the doctor."

"Don't be silly," Christy said. "We just wanted to say hello and meet the children."

Three barefoot children gathered in front of Christy with nervous smiles. "This here's Louise," Curtis said. "She's fifteen. John is ten. And Hannah just turned eight last week."

"Etta's in the cradle inside," Margaret added.

"And this here's Violet," Hannah said, pulling a small brown field mouse from her pocket. "I rescued her from an owl. She lost one foot, but I fixed her up good as new."

"Hannah's got a way with animals," Margaret said.

"All the children's been to school some," Curtis added proudly. "Louise could practically read better 'n her own teacher."

"Wonderful!" Christy exclaimed. "Most of the children at the mission school haven't had much schooling. There are so many of them that I often ask the better students to help out. It'll be wonderful to have you there, Louise."

"Do you have a library?" Louise asked hopefully.

"Unfortunately, no. Our school just manages to scrape by on donations. But we do the best we can." Christy smiled. "And if you want more practice reading, we have a Bible reading every week at the mission. Maybe you and your mother would like to come."

"We'd be right honored," Margaret said.

Just then, a branch snapped in the woods. Curtis spun around, gun raised, searching the trees.

"It's nothin', Curtis," Margaret said gently. She sighed. "He'll put himself in an early grave, fussin' and worryin' himself this way."

"Curtis," the doctor asked, "what was it you were going to show me?"

"I was fixin' to bury it when you all showed up," Curtis replied. "Follow me."

He led them to the back of the house and pointed. On the ground near a half-dug hole lay a dead skunk. Its stomach had been slit open. White maggots squirmed over the gaping wound. The stench was horrendous.

"That," Curtis said, "was waitin' for us on our

porch this mornin'. Nice welcomin' present, don't you think?"

"Poor ol' skunk," muttered Hannah.

"Poor ol' us, you mean," said John. "That skunk's a warnin'. It's sayin' 'get lost.'" He crossed his arms over his chest. "Told you we shoulda stayed put. At least back home we knowed who our enemies was."

Margaret patted John's head. "Your pa wanted to get 'way from the city, John. Try his hand at farmin'."

"There's better farm land all over the place. It's too hilly here."

"Come on, everyone." Curtis gestured toward the front yard. "I'll take care of this later."

"Where did you move here from, Curtis?" Christy asked as they settled on the front porch of the cabin.

"Virginia. Fredericksburg, to be exact. Nice enough place, but it had its share of skunks, too, if'n you know what I mean."

"And what brought you to Cutter Gap, if you don't mind my asking?"

"Long story," Curtis said, smiling.

"My great-grandpa's why," Hannah volunteered. "Tell her, Pa."

"My grandpa, William, passed through these parts a long, long time ago," Curtis said. "Five years before the Civil War, in fact. He was a slave who escaped from a plantation in Alabama. Made it all the way to Philadelphia, safe and sound, with some help. He always had a kind word to say about some folks in Cutter Gap, Tennessee— how they took him in and did right by him. How the mountains made you feel like the Lord was your next-door neighbor." He paused, staring off at the green peaks capped by golden sunlight. "So when we was lookin' to move on, this place came into my head. It was like my grandpa was tellin' me where to go."

"And once Curtis gets an idea in his head, you watch out!" Margaret said, laughing.

"I wanted to get away from the city, find me some land. And I liked the idea of bein' so plumb high that heaven's just that much closer, if'n I needed to do some talkin'." He laughed. "Anyways, a friend of mine knew a man who traveled to El Pano regular. And that man knew Ben Pentland, the mailman."

"And Ben knew I'd been thinking of selling part of my land to help buy some more medical supplies," the doctor finished.

"Well, we're awfully glad to have you here," Christy said.

John kicked at a rock angrily. "You be the only ones."

"John," Margaret said, "don't you be rude to your new teacher."

"I'm afraid John's right to be on guard," the doctor said. "I just talked to Bob Allen, your neighbor on the west side. He runs the little mill on Blackberry Creek." Doctor MacNeill gave a grim smile. "Let's just say this is going to take Bob some time to get used to."

"Should we be . . . worried, Doctor?" Margaret asked.

"I don't know, to be honest. Most of the people here are good, Margaret. But they take a long time to warm up to strangers, and they don't take kindly to new ideas. I'd be careful for a while. If you ever need anything, you know where to find me."

"And we'll always be there for you at the mission," Christy added.

"That's a start, anyway," Curtis said.

"Well, we should get going," Christy said. "I hope to see you children in school soon!"

"Thank you both for stoppin' by," Curtis said. "We'll have you over proper-like as soon as we get ourselves settled."

Christy and the doctor had just started down the path when they heard someone running after them.

"Miz Teacher?"

Christy turned to see Hannah rushing toward them. "What is it, Hannah?"

"I was wonderin' . . ." The little girl smiled shyly. She had huge, dark eyes fringed by long lashes. "I was wonderin' if'n you have any eight-year-olds at your school."

"Why, we have lots!" Christy exclaimed.

"Girls?"

"Plenty of girls."

"You s'pose . . ."

"Do I suppose what?"

"You s'pose you got any eight-year-old girls who'd be needin' a friend?" Hannah asked casually.

"I'm sure we'll find one for you," Christy said gently.

Hannah grinned. "I was hopin' so!"

Christy looked at Doctor MacNeill as Hannah ran off. "I just hope I'm right."

"So do I," the doctor said, shaking his head.

❧ Five ❧

That evening, Christy joined Alice Henderson in the mission house parlor for a cup of tea.

"You seem troubled, Christy," Miss Alice said.

"I can't seem to stop thinking about the Washingtons," Christy said. "I'm so worried the people here won't accept them."

She looked at Miss Alice hopefully. Alice Henderson was a Quaker mission worker who'd helped to found the school. She was a lovely, dignified woman, generous, thoughtful, and strong. Many times since coming here, Christy had turned to Miss Alice for help in understanding the people of Cutter Gap. She always seemed to have an answer, and her answers always carried a message of hope. She was known throughout the mountain communities and highly respected by all.

But tonight Miss Alice's deep gray eyes were troubled. "I wish I could tell you that these people will come to accept the Washingtons. I wish I could tell you that when they read in their Bibles 'Thou shalt love thy neighbor as thyself,' they will take those words into their hearts and act on them." She sipped at her tea. "But I don't know if that will happen, Christy. It may take years. It may even take lifetimes."

"I'm worried about the children at school. They can be so cruel sometimes. And some of the older boys, like Lundy . . . they can be downright dangerous."

Miss Alice nodded. "I've heard some talk about parents who plan to keep their children out of school if the Washingtons come."

"I suppose all we can do is try to help the children see that we're all really the same on the inside. In time, maybe they'll come to understand that."

"I hope we can say the same of their parents," said Miss Alice. "Sometimes it's easier for children to see the truth of things." She reached for the teapot. "More tea?"

"No, thanks. I should be getting to bed before long."

"You've had a long day. Thank you for picking up that medicine from Doctor MacNeill."

"I didn't mind."

"No," Miss Alice said with a knowing smile, "I don't suppose you did."

Christy went to the window. The stars glimmered over the dark trees like a thousand fireflies.

"Miss Alice?" Christy said. "What would you say if somebody wanted you to pretend to be something you're not?"

Miss Alice gazed at Christy thoughtfully. "Would that somebody be a certain physician who shall, for our purposes, remain nameless?"

Christy grinned. "Am I that transparent?"

"As glass."

"Neil told one of his old school chums that he and I are engaged. Now that friend is getting married, and Neil wants me to go to the wedding."

"As his fiancée?"

"As his rich fiancée who speaks four languages when she isn't busy winning waltz championships with him."

Miss Alice laughed. She had a glorious laugh, like bells ringing, that always made Christy feel better about life. Instantly, Christy found herself laughing, too, so hard it brought tears to her eyes.

"It is . . ." Christy gasped, "it is pretty ridiculous, when you think about it, isn't it?"

"Neil MacNeill!" Miss Alice said, chuckling. "The most down-to-earth, no-nonsense man I've ever met, caught up in a story that silly? Yes, I'd say it's quite ridiculous."

Christy wiped her eyes. "I told him I simply couldn't lie like that. What else *could* I have said?"

Still smiling, Miss Alice considered for a moment. "Don't worry, Christy. Neil is a reasonable man. If I know him as well as I think I do, he'll come to his senses and see the error of his ways."

"I think he was feeling a little jealous of his friend. James has all the things Neil has had to sacrifice—money, a thriving practice, a nice home."

"That's understandable. Jealousy is a perfectly human emotion. However, this little deception of Neil's is . . . well, it's going a bit too far."

"I'll tell him I'll go to the wedding, but only on the condition that he tell the truth," Christy said.

"It's certainly easier than learning three new languages overnight," Miss Alice said with a grin.

David appeared in the doorway. "What on earth are you two giggling about?"

"Men," Christy replied.

David raised his brows. "Oh? Anyone I know?"

"Actually," said Miss Alice, "he doesn't sound a bit like anyone we know. But we're hoping that will change."

Up in her bedroom, Christy climbed under her blanket with a sigh. She graded papers for a while. Then she pulled out her diary from her nightstand. She wanted to jot down the day's events before she drifted off to sleep:

I confronted two problems today. One, I think I can handle. Doctor MacNeill seems to be going through some doubts about his life here, but I'm sure he'll come to see how much he belongs in Cutter Gap. He has to. If he were to leave, the Cove would suffer terribly without a doctor. And I have to admit that I would suffer, too.

The other problem is very different. A new family has moved here, and it's already clear they aren't going to get a warm reception. Somehow, I have to find a way to help the Washingtons. Miss Alice says it will take time for them to be accepted, maybe years. But I'm determined to find a way to help them put down roots here. If I keep my eyes and my heart open, perhaps, God willing, I'll see the way.

❧ Six ❧

Della May settled into her desk at school the next morning, carefully sneaking a peek at her brother Creed. He winked at her, then put a finger to his lips. She knew he'd hidden Scalawag in his desk. She also knew that if Miz Christy found out, she'd be mad as a skinned snake.

On Miz Christy's very first day of teaching, Creed had brought Scalawag to school. She'd made Creed promise not to bring the raccoon again, and Creed had kept his promise until today. It wasn't like Creed had a choice. Scalawag had been acting plumb strange, moping and refusing to eat. He usually followed Creed around like a hound dog, but lately, he'd taken to slipping out of the Allens' cabin at night, heading off to who knows where.

This morning, when Scalawag wouldn't even eat the fresh possum meat Creed had saved for him, Creed had decided the only thing to do was take the raccoon along to school, hidden in a burlap sack.

There were six Allen children altogether, but Della May was the only one Creed had told about Scalawag. He knew he could trust her. They were almost like best friends, although Della May sometimes wished she had a *real* best friend. Brothers didn't really count. She always had Wanda Beck and Mary O'Teale, but neither of them liked to read the way Della May did, or just sit quietly in the woods and watch the animals and birds come and go.

Della May loved Creed, but sometimes he could be a bit of a troublemaker. She spent an awful lot of time pulling him out of one scrape or another. And she had a feeling today was going to be one of those days.

If Miz Christy found out about Scalawag, she'd be hopping mad. She might even tell their pa, and he'd been mad enough all on his own lately, fretting about the new folks down the road. Della May shuddered a little, just remembering how dark and mean his eyes had been yesterday.

Truth was, a lot of pas and mas were fretting lately. Many of Della May's schoolmates were missing today, on account of they heard the

Washingtons were coming to school. Her own pa had wanted to keep the children home, but Creed and Della May had begged and pleaded until he'd covered his ears and said "Be off with you, then," in a growly voice.

Suddenly a hush fell over the room. Creed nudged her with his elbow.

In the doorway stood Miz Christy, the preacher, and a woman Della May had never seen before. She was wearing a blue dress like Della May's ma wore sometimes, tattered at the edges, but clean. She had a smile like Della May's ma, too, the shy kind. But her skin was nothing like Della May had ever seen before. It was a warm brown acorn color.

"Her skin . . ." Della may whispered to Creed, "it's so purty."

Creed sent her a hush-your-mouth look, and Della May realized she must have said something very wrong.

The ma stepped aside and some children came into the room. There were three of them, a girl and a boy, both older than Della May, and another girl, who looked to be just about eight. The older children had a proud look in their eyes, but the youngest girl just looked scared and hoping all at once.

She met Della May's eyes. Della May started to smile, then stopped herself. She knew for a fact *that* would be wrong. Her pa had taught her that much.

"Pheww!" Lundy Taylor cried. "Somethin's stinkin' awful! Lordamercy, what *is* that smell?"

Some of the children giggled. Miz Christy's face turned hard as stone. The little girl moved closer to her ma. Della May wondered if the girl was going to cry.

"That will be enough, Lundy," the preacher scolded. Della May had never heard him sound so angry. "Quite enough."

"Children," Christy said, "I'm very pleased to introduce you to some new students who'll be joining us today. The Washingtons have just moved to a place between Doctor MacNeill's cabin and the Allens'. This is Louise, who's fifteen. John is ten. And Hannah is eight."

"They don't belong in this school," one of the older boys muttered. "They's too stupid. Their kind got the brains of a half-wit rabbit."

"Who said that?" Christy demanded.

Nobody spoke. Della May sneaked a glance at the girl named Hannah. No, she wasn't crying. But she looked right scared. Della May wondered how it would feel if Lundy and the older boys were saying those things about her. They'd made fun of her sometimes, the way they did all the younger children. That was bad enough. But this talk had a meanness to it, sharp as a knife.

Della May knew that if she was Hannah, she'd probably be crying buckets by now. But maybe these people were different. Maybe they didn't have the same kind of feelings as white folks.

"I want to make one thing clear from the start." Christy went to the front of the schoolroom. "That kind of thing will not be tolerated in this room under any circumstances. The next person who speaks that way will be sent home from school for a week. And if it happens again, that person will be expelled."

"Teacher?" Della May's brother, Little Burl, raised his hand. "What's ''spelled'?"

"*Expelled*. It means you can't ever come back to school again, Little Burl."

The preacher walked over to the big boys in the back of the room. He had a dark look on his face, worse even than when he was preachin' up a storm on Sunday mornings. He talked to the boys in a low voice. Della May couldn't hear the words. But she could sure tell he meant business.

Her pa had said it would be this way. The mission people siding with the Washingtons. Acting like they belonged here same as decent white folks. He'd said Miz Christy and Miz Alice and the preacher would be full of tales, just like Doctor MacNeill, but that the children shouldn't believe a word they said.

Christy searched the room. "We need to get you children settled," she said.

Della May sank lower in her seat. There was an empty desk right next to her.

"Louise and John, there's a bench on the left side available. And Hannah, why don't you take that desk next to Della May, right over there?"

Some of the children snickered. A few moved their desks.

Della May looked around helplessly. There was nowhere for her to move. She was trapped.

"You'll be all right," Creed advised. "Just pretend she ain't there."

While Christy said goodbye to the preacher and Mrs. Washington, the girl named Hannah slowly approached the empty desk beside Della May.

"You be Della May?" she asked in a soft voice.

Della May gave a nod, staring straight ahead.

"Then I guess this is where I'm supposed to be sittin'."

Della May tried to pretend she wasn't there, just like Creed had suggested. But it was awfully hard to pretend a living, breathing person was invisible.

"Maybe you and I could be friends," Hannah said. And then something deep inside told Della May it was going to be impossible to pretend that Hannah Washington wasn't there.

❧ Seven ❧

Hannah slipped into the desk. Della May sneaked a peek at her. Hannah had the same pretty brown skin as her ma. Her hair was caught up in two pigtails, tied with red ribbons. It was sparkly and dark and springy. Magical hair.

"Want to see my pet mouse?" Hannah asked in a soft whisper-voice.

Della May shook her head no. She could feel the eyes of the other students on her.

"Maybe later," Hannah said.

Della May ignored her. Behind her, she heard the sound of desks and benches scraping.

Della May looked at Creed. He shrugged. There was nowhere for him to shove his desk.

He opened the lid a crack. Scalawag's wet black nose poked out. Quickly Creed closed the desk, but not before Hannah noticed Scalawag.

"You got somethin' in there?" she asked Creed. "Can I see?"

Creed shook his head no.

Christy went to the blackboard. "We're going to start the day with a discussion of your arithmetic papers." A few students groaned. "Which, I am sorry to say, were not very impressive. Let's start with a review of addition."

She picked up a piece of chalk. It squeaked as she wrote numbers in a long column on the board.

"Creed Allen?" Christy called. "Why don't you come up here and help me with this problem?"

"I don't rightly like sums, factually speakin'," Creed said.

"That's exactly why I asked you," Christy said with a grin.

Creed looked over at Della May, worry in his bright blue eyes. He pointed to his desk. Della May nodded.

"The rest of you," Christy said, "work the problem at your desks."

Creed went to the board. He scratched his head, then took the chalk and went to work. Christy watched, her back to the class.

Della May reached for her little, cracked blackboard. The class fell quiet as the students worked, heads bowed, on the problem.

Suddenly, Della May felt a hand touch her shoulder. She jumped when she realized it was Hannah. How dare that girl touch her! She started to protest, but Hannah pointed her finger at Creed's desk.

The lid was opening! Scalawag poked out his head and blinked.

Della May tried to push him back, but he was in no mood to take orders. In a flash, he slipped out of the desk and leapt straight into her lap. Frantically, she held the struggling raccoon in her arms.

She had to get rid of him, and fast! But where was she going to put him? The lid on her own desk was broken.

She glanced around the room. Everyone was working. Miz Christy's back was still to the class.

"You're on the right track, Creed," Christy said. "Keep at it."

With one arm clutching Scalawag, Della May reached over to open the lid on Creed's desk. Scalawag squirmed out of her arms, straight into Hannah's lap.

Della May gasped. Now Miz Christy was sure to find out!

"Almost, Creed," Miz Christy was saying. "Can anyone tell me where he made his mistake?"

Scalawag was sitting quietly in Hannah's arms. She stroked him behind the ears, whispering something. Then she slipped him into her desk, easy as pie, just as Miz Christy turned around.

Hannah grinned at Della May, a big, I've-got-a-secret grin. She raised her hand.

She's going to tell, Della May thought, her heart galloping inside her like a frightened colt.

"I think Creed forgot to carry the one," Hannah said, calm and cool as could be. "So the seven should be an eight."

"Very good, Hannah," Christy said.

Della May stared at Hannah, her jaw dropped in disbelief. Hannah gave her a little wink.

"You can sneak him back later," Hannah whispered.

Della May didn't answer. For the life of her, she didn't know what to say.

—◦—◦—

When it came time for the noon dinner spell, Creed and Della May and Hannah waited until everyone else had left the schoolroom.

As soon as it was safe, Hannah opened her desk and lifted Scalawag into her arms. "He's a fine pet," she said, stroking the raccoon's head. Scalawag made a soft purring noise.

"Give him," Creed snapped. "He ain't yours."

"Creed," Della May said, "like I told you, she hid him for me. Miz Christy woulda seen him for sure if'n Hannah hadn't . . ." Her voice trailed off.

"Here you go," Hannah said, carefully placing Scalawag into Creed's arms. "Does it have a name?"

Creed shrugged. "Scalawag's his name. But don't you be tellin' anyone 'bout him, hear?"

"He's awful quiet," Hannah said.

"He's been feelin' poorly," Della May said, scratching the raccoon's ears. She realized with a start that she was talking to Hannah, just like she was a regular person.

Suddenly Scalawag struggled out of Creed's grasp. The little raccoon scampered over the desktops. He stopped by an open window, sniffed the air, then bounded outside.

"Scalawag!" Creed cried. "Come back!"

The three children dashed down the front steps of the school to the side yard. Scalawag was nowhere to be seen.

"He coulda gone anywheres," Creed moaned. "I'll never find him now."

"Raccoons are right smart about things. He'll come back, I'll bet you," Hannah said as she searched under some bushes.

"Ain't like him to run away," Creed said. "He just ain't been hisself lately."

Della May patted her brother's back. She could tell he was about to cry. "Don't fret yourself," she said. "Scalawag's your best friend. He'll come back. He probably just didn't like all that 'rithmetic, is all."

Creed frowned at Hannah. "Didn't like somethin', that's for sure and certain."

Della May watched her brother stomp off. It wasn't fair, exactly, blaming Hannah. She'd done her best to hide old Scalawag, after all. And Creed had been the one holding him when he'd run off.

She looked at Hannah uncertainly. "It weren't your fault," she said at last.

Hannah smiled a little. "I know. He was just bein' ornery. Got me a brother just like him. Feisty as a stepped-on bee sometimes."

Della May tried not to smile back, but she couldn't help it.

"Creed's all right. Most of the time."

"My brother John is all right most of the time, too. It's those *other* times that'll try your patience."

Quiet fell between them. Della May felt all twisted up and funny inside. She could almost hear her pa yellin' over her shoulder about how she shouldn't be talking to Hannah. But she sure seemed nice enough.

Maybe she'd just keep up her guard, to be on the safe side. See how things went. Granny Allen had a Bible quote she was always saying—"By their fruits ye shall know them."

Della May figured that meant she should give Hannah a chance. Judge her by the way she acted, not just by what others say, or the color of her skin.

In the meantime, she wouldn't say anything to her pa. No point in getting him angry and all riled up.

❧ Eight ❧

That afternoon, Christy rode over to Doctor MacNeill's cabin on Prince, the mission's black stallion.

The doctor was on his porch when Christy rode up. "So," he asked, "did the Washington children come to school today?"

Christy gave a terse nod.

"I'm almost afraid to ask how it went."

She climbed off Prince and tied him to a tree. "Let me put it this way. It was a long day. Longer still for those poor children."

"I'm sorry to say I'm not surprised."

"The older boys threatened them all day. Even when they didn't use their voices, I could see it in their eyes. And the younger children—well, they just acted as if Louise and John and Hannah were invisible."

"Give them time. They may come around."

"That's what Miss Alice said. But I'm starting to have my doubts."

"Come on in and sit awhile. You look worn out. What brings you here, anyway? Not that it matters. I'm always glad to see you."

Christy climbed the porch steps. "Well, Miss Alice asked me to pick up some more cough medicine. She's afraid two bottles won't be enough." She leaned against the door jamb, smiling. "That could have waited, I suppose. The other reason I'm here is to tell you I've decided to accept your kind offer to attend the wedding."

Doctor MacNeill brushed his hand through his hair. He gazed at her doubtfully. "Are you saying you'll go along with my little plan?"

"No. I'm saying I'll go if you'll agree to tell James the whole truth."

The doctor sighed. "You drive a hard bargain, Miss Huddleston."

"You'd have to tell him the truth eventually, Neil."

"I know. I know. You're right. I suppose this rivalry seems small-minded to you. Didn't you ever compete with a friend?"

"Mary Ellen Lanning." Christy settled into the doctor's old rocking chair. "She stole Gus Ricketts from me."

"Your first love?" the doctor asked.

"You might say so. I was all of twelve years old. But I was still heartbroken."

The doctor pulled up a chair beside her. "Imagine the jealousy you felt toward Mary Ellen Lanning, and multiply it by a thousand." He shook his head. "I know I shouldn't feel this way. I made my choice to live here. I ought to be happy with it. And I realize it's wrong to envy what James has. But still . . . don't you ever look at those seventy youngsters in your class and wonder if you'd be happier somewhere else? If you're really making a difference in their lives?"

Christy stared out the window. Two mockingbirds were making a ruckus as they chased each other through the sky. "Of course I feel frustrated, Neil. Especially on days like today, when I can't see any way to get through to those children. But there are good days, too—days when there is laughter and singing, instead of arguing and fighting. I try to concentrate on those."

"But the fighting doesn't ever really stop, that's the point. I patch up a man's wound so he can go right back to feuding. I sell land to some good people, hoping they'll be able to put down roots. And to what end? So they can be persecuted till they're forced to leave?" He rubbed his eyes.

Christy's heart ached at the pain in Neil's voice. She'd felt the same way many times, especially after she'd first come to Cutter Gap to teach. But it was harder to see someone she cared about suffer through the same despair and doubt.

She squeezed his hand. "Believe me, Neil. God brought you back to Cutter Gap for a reason."

"I wish I had your faith." He shrugged, forcing a smile. "But enough of this. We have some practicing to do."

"Practicing?"

"Even waltz champions need a little practice now and then."

"You know, I seem to remember that on our recent trip to Asheville, you weren't nearly so enthusiastic about dancing."

"That dance at the Barclays'?" The doctor groaned. "You were too busy dancing with your old beau, Lance, as I recall. The reverend and I stood in the corner all night like a couple of wallflowers. But I danced with you at the mission open house."

"That's true. I regained the use of my toes after a few weeks."

"Actually, you said I was a wonderful dancer. And remember that night we danced alone by the fire, after you rescued Ruby Mae Morrison?"

"Yes," Christy said softly. "That I will never forget."

"No broken toes?"

"None whatsoever."

The doctor stood and held out his hand. "I won't forget it, either," he said.

Christy gave a little curtsy. "I'll only dance if you promise to hum a *real* waltz."

"Strauss, then. Just for you."

Taking Christy's hand, the doctor led her out to the front yard. Slowly they spun around the grass in graceful circles while the doctor softly hummed.

It was so pleasant. Christy tried to forget about all the troubles that day. She tried to focus on the doctor's low, soft voice. The sun, warm on her shoulders. The wind, making the trees whisper secrets. The air, heavy with the smell of honeysuckle.

But every time she closed her eyes, she saw the frightened but determined faces of the Washington children. And the ugly faces of hatred on too many of her other students.

Suddenly the pleasant calm was interrupted by the sharp sound of gunshots.

One. Two. Three. Four.

Christy stopped cold. "It's coming from the direction of the Washingtons'!"

"Get Prince. I'll grab my gun."

Christy untied Prince's reins. The doctor bounded from his cabin. In one hand was his gun. In the other was his medical bag. He strapped the gun and his bag behind Prince's saddle, then leapt onto the stallion.

He took Christy's hand and lifted her up. "Hang on," he instructed as she settled behind him.

She wrapped her arms around his chest. They headed down the path toward the Washingtons' as fast as possible, dodging low tree limbs and bushes along the way.

They'd almost reached the cabin when they saw Hannah running toward them, waving her arms frantically.

"They shot John!" she cried. "They shot my brother!"

❧ Nine ❧

When Christy and the doctor reached the Washingtons' front porch, they found Margaret and Louise tending to John. His right arm was bleeding just above the elbow.

"Ain't nothin' but a scratch," John said. His voice was calm, but Christy could see the terror in his eyes.

"Scratch!" Margaret said furiously. "A few more inches the wrong way and it coulda killed you!"

Doctor MacNeill and Christy climbed off Prince. She retrieved the medical bag while the doctor examined John's arm.

"What happened, Hannah?" Christy asked.

"Ain't sure." Hannah's lower lip trembled. "Me and John was in the yard. All of a sudden we heard someone in the woods out yonder. They started firin', and we went runnin'. I fell in the dirt. Violet was in my pocket. Nearly crushed the poor ol' thing."

"You've just got a flesh wound, John," Doctor MacNeill said. "You're a lucky boy."

"Lucky," John repeated bitterly. "Yes, sir. I s'pose I'm lucky they didn't kill me outright."

"How could anyone do this?" Margaret demanded. "We haven't bothered anyone. This is our land, right and proper."

Hannah tugged on Christy's arm. "Why would somebody go shootin' at me and John, Teacher? I done tried to make friends at school today."

"I know you did, Hannah." Christy knelt beside the little girl. "Did you see who was shooting? Do you have any idea who did this?"

"Thought I seen a gray horse back in the woods," Hannah said. "But it's hard to say."

Christy exchanged a glance with the doctor. Bob Allen owned a dapple gray mare.

"Where's your father, Hannah?" the doctor asked as he cleaned John's wound.

"Ran up the path lookin' for the men."

"With his gun," Margaret added anxiously.

"That could mean trouble," the doctor said. "Christy, would you finish bandaging John's arm? I'm going to try to catch up with Curtis before there's any more shooting."

"I'm going with you," Christy said firmly.

"There's no point in you—"

"I'm going," Christy repeated.

Doctor MacNeill sighed. "Fine. I know better than to argue with you. Margaret, there are bandages in my bag. Apply one to John's wound with a little pressure. We'll be back as soon as we can."

"Be careful," Margaret said.

Christy and Doctor MacNeill climbed onto Prince. The doctor kept his shotgun at the ready, while Christy scanned the dense woods for any movement.

"You're thinking what I'm thinking, aren't you?" Christy said as they headed up the shady path.

"That you're the most incredibly stubborn woman in Tennessee and I shouldn't have let you ride along with me?"

"That Bob Allen's behind this."

Doctor MacNeill nodded. "Not that we'd ever be able to prove it. But yes. I'd bet my last dollar it was Bob. He could have been alone, but my guess is he brought along some help." They heard a noise in the bushes. Christy stiffened. By now she recognized all too well the metallic click of a shotgun being cocked.

"Hold it right there!" a low voice cried from somewhere in the underbrush.

"Curtis?" the doctor called. He brought Prince to a stop. "Is that you? It's me, Doctor MacNeill."

Slowly Curtis emerged from the woods, his gun at the ready. "They shot my boy, Doc," he said. "I gotta find the men who done it."

"Curtis, I understand how you feel," the doctor said. "But it's not going to help your family one bit if you walk into an ambush up the path."

"So you're sayin' just let it pass? Let the white folks shoot my boy and laugh about it?"

"No. I'm saying let Christy and me try to deal with these people. Calm them down, talk some sense into them."

"They shot my boy, Doctor—"

"John's fine. It was just a minor flesh wound."

"So that makes it all right?" Curtis demanded, his voice choked with rage. "Why should I listen to you? How can you talk that way? Whose side are you on, anyway?"

"Nobody's more upset about this than Doctor MacNeill, Curtis," Christy said gently. "And if anybody can talk some reason into these men, it's the doctor."

Curtis shook his head. "Ain't no reasonin' with hate."

"The doctor sold you that land because he thought you could make a home here. He thought the people of Cutter Gap were ready for a change," Christy said. "Give him a chance to make things right. You head on home and tend to John."

Curtis exhaled slowly. He stared off into the trees, considering. "All right, then. I'll do what you say, Miz Christy. But if anyone comes near my children again, they'll be answerin' to the barrel of a gun."

"I'll stop by later to check on John," the doctor promised.

They rode on in silence for a few minutes. "You may be stubborn," the doctor said, turning back to smile at Christy, "but you're also persuasive."

"That's not all," Christy said jokingly. "I speak four languages, too."

"Impressive," the doctor said as they approached the Allens' cabin. He reined Prince to a halt. "You may need all four to get through to Bob. Why don't you wait here till I check things out?"

"I know Bob and Mary Allen very well, Neil. And if Creed or Rob or Festus are mixed up in this, I'll have as good a chance as you of calming things down."

"All right, then. Stay a safe distance behind me, at least."

They dismounted and stepped into the clearing. The cabin was quiet, and so was the little mill beyond. The only sound was the babble of Blackberry Creek as it rushed past.

Bob's mare was in front of the cabin. There was foam on her mouth, as if she'd been running hard. Christy touched the mare's flank as she passed. It was damp with sweat.

Suddenly, the cabin door flew open. Bob appeared, his shotgun in the crook of his arm. "Howdy, Doc. Miz Christy. What brings you to our neck o' the woods?"

"John Washington's been shot," the doctor said. "But then, you already knew that, didn't you, Bob?"

✣ Ten ✣

Don't know what you're speakin' of, Doctor MacNeill."

"Put the gun down, Bob. We need to talk."

"If'n you come here about them no-accounts, I got nothin' to say to you. You come for socializin', then you're welcome."

Doctor MacNeill pointed his own gun right at Bob's chest. "I've come," he boomed, "to warn you that if you go near those people again, I'll—"

Christy put her hand on the doctor's arm to silence him. "Bob," she said sweetly, "I think I'll take you up on your kindly offer. I haven't seen Mary in such a long time. And how is Granny Allen doing?"

Without waiting, Christy marched up the front steps, walking right between the two guns each man had trained on the other. She brushed past a stunned Bob without even blinking.

At the door she spun around. "Coming, Doctor MacNeill?" she called.

"Might as well head on inside, Doc." Bob gestured with his gun toward the door. "Confounded women! Don't give no stock in argufyin' the way we men does."

Mary, Granny, and the Allen children were waiting in the cramped, dark cabin. "Come in, come in," Mary said, taking Christy's hand. She was a stooped, graying woman who looked much older than her years. "All this fussin' and carryin' on! Like to make a body plumb wore out."

Christy took a seat at the table, and Della May and Little Burl gathered close. The doctor stood in the doorway, his face set in a stony grimace. Bob leaned against the far wall, arms crossed over his chest. In the corner, Granny Allen sat in a wooden rocker. She was a tiny woman, well into her eighties, with a toothless smile and hands gnarled by rheumatism.

Silence fell in the crowded room. "Where's Creed?" Christy asked, to break the quiet.

"Mopin' out by the creek," Della May said.

"Moping?" Christy repeated. "Why?"

"Scalawag's done disappeared. Can't find him nowheres."

"When did he disappear?"

"Oh, that's hard to say," Della May replied a little evasively.

"He'll turn up," Granny said loudly. She was slightly deaf and tended to yell. "Mark my word."

Mary cleared her throat. "Could I fix y'all somethin' to eat?"

"This isn't a social call, Mary," the doctor said firmly, eyes locked on Bob. "This is about what just happened at the Washingtons' place. A young boy was shot."

"Shame, ain't it?" Bob said, with a hint of a sneer.

Della May and Little Burl looked at the floor, as if they were afraid to meet Christy's eyes.

"You did it, didn't you, Bob?" the doctor said.

"Prove it," Bob challenged.

"Your horse was seen there."

"That don't prove nothin'."

"Bob," Christy said, "Curtis Washington was on his way over here to even the score. The doctor and I stopped him. But next time, you might not be so lucky. We need to stop this madness before it turns into a war."

"That's a war I'd win," Bob grinned. "Purty much everybody's on my side, 'ceptin' you mission folks."

"Haven't you had enough fighting to last a lifetime?" Christy cried. "The Taylors and your clan have been feuding for generations.

Why do you need another enemy? Look what you're teaching your children."

"Teachin' 'em the way o' the world, is all," Mary said softly.

"But it doesn't have to be this way," Christy said. "The Washingtons are good people. Why can't you give them a chance? I invited Margaret and Louise to our next Bible study. You'll see then, Mary."

"She ain't goin' to no Bible readin', not if they be there!" Bob shouted.

"But I like goin' . . ." Mary said. "I get so lonely here. And Miss Alice makes us tea and reads Scripture to us—"

"You ain't goin', woman!" Bob screamed.

"Hush, Bob," Granny said. "You're a-hurtin' my ears, and I'm purt-near stone deaf. Let Mary go to the Bible study, if'n she wants."

"Didn't you hear? You want her near them two women that ain't our own kind? I won't have it, I'm a-tellin' you!" Bob pounded his fist on the wall. He beat it so hard that a needlepoint stitching in a crude frame—the only decoration in the cabin— fell to the floor. The frame splintered and broke apart.

"My stitchin'!" Granny moaned.

Christy picked up the faded fabric. The alphabet was carefully embroidered on it. The date "1841" had been sewn into the corner. Instead of a signature, like the other needlepoints

Christy had seen, Granny had stitched a tiny bluebird.

"This is beautiful, Granny," Christy said.

"Made it when I was just a wee thing," Granny said.

"I'm powerful sorry, Granny," Bob said, hanging his head like a guilty child. "I'm sure I can mend the frame."

Granny looked at him sharply through clouded blue eyes. "I'll tell you what you can mend. You can let that wife o' yours go to the Bible readin', just like always. I'd go myself, if'n I was a little more spry."

"But—"

"Hush! I've had mules with more sense than you, Bob Allen. Mary wants to go, she'll go."

Bob frowned. "Women!" he muttered.

"Bob, we haven't settled this," Doctor MacNeill said. "Next time I hear you've been near the Washingtons, I'll be using my gun. And I won't stop to socialize first. You understand me?"

"I understand you started this whole miserable mess," Bob shot back. "And I understand one other thing. You, Miz Christy, Miz Alice, the preacher, maybe two or three others are on the Washingtons' side. But I got me the whole o' Cutter Gap on my side. Who do you think is gonna win that war, Doc? We'll get you and those Washingtons. You started somethin' you ain't able to finish. You done forgot your roots, Doc. You're as much a part of this place as the rest of us."

In two great steps, Doctor MacNeill placed himself squarely in front of Bob. He grabbed him by the shirt and shoved him hard against the wall.

Della May cried out. Mary gasped, her hand to her mouth.

"Don't you threaten me, Bob Allen," the doctor said between gritted teeth. "That's a fight you don't want. And don't you talk to me about my roots. Right about now, I'm embarrassed to be from this place."

Christy touched the doctor's shoulder. "Neil. Come on."

Doctor MacNeill released Bob, who slumped against the wall, rubbing his neck. "Traitor," Bob growled.

The doctor stomped out the door. Christy started to follow, then hesitated. "Come to the Bible study, Mary," she said. "Please."

When Mary didn't answer, Christy knew there was nothing more to say.

⚞ Eleven ⚟

On Monday during the noon break, Christy sat with David on the front steps of the mission school. The children were spread all over the lawn, lazing under the trees while they ate.

"So, any problems so far today?" asked David, who taught Bible study at the school and helped with arithmetic classes when he had time.

"Somebody put molasses on Louise Washington's chair while she was writing on the chalkboard. I tried, but I couldn't find the culprit. I'm pretty sure it was Lundy, though," Christy sighed. "I just can't seem to get through to these children, David."

"Join the club." David gave an understanding laugh. "How do you think I felt yesterday, during my sermon about brotherly love and tolerance?"

"It was a wonderful sermon, David."

"Too bad the church was only half full."

"I keep thinking if I could just get one or two of the children to make friends with the Washingtons, that would be a good start. I thought I saw Della May whispering to Hannah this morning, but I was probably imagining things. Given the way Bob Allen feels, it's difficult to imagine one of his own children defying him that way."

"It's hard for these children to take a stand like that," David pointed out. "It takes real bravery to go against your family and friends and do the right thing."

He pointed to Creed Allen, who was sitting under a tree, head in his hands. "Speaking of the Allens, what's wrong with Creed? He's been so quiet lately."

"Scalawag ran away," Christy explained.

"Oh, that explains it. Poor kid. Speaking of running away, I hear you're planning a trip with Doctor MacNeill."

"Word travels fast."

"You're going to a wedding?" David asked, brows raised.

"We'll see. If things don't settle down around here, I'm not sure I'll be comfortable leaving, even if it's only for a couple days. Miss Alice did say she wouldn't mind filling in at the school."

"I'll help out, too, if I can. Although I'd

prefer it," David added with a grin, "if you were going to a wedding with me."

Before Christy could reply, a sharp cry rang out. "Miz Christy, Preacher, come quick!" Ruby Mae called. "John and Lundy's a-fightin'!"

Christy and David ran to the other side of the school. A small group of students had circled around John and Lundy. John was on the ground. Lundy straddled his chest.

"Tell me, you slime-belly snake!" Lundy screamed. "Tell me what you did with it!"

"I don't know what you're a-talkin' about. I swear it!" John shouted.

Lundy raised his fist to strike. Just in the nick of time, David grabbed his arm. Together he and Christy yanked Lundy off John.

"Lundy Taylor!" Christy cried. "What do you think you're doing?"

"He stole my hat!" Lundy screamed. "Stole it right off my desk when I weren't lookin'."

"I didn't take his fool hat," John said as he climbed to his feet shakily. "What would I want with that dirty ol'—"

"I'm goin' to pummel you good for that!" Lundy started for John, but David held him back.

"Did anyone see John take Lundy's hat?" Christy asked.

Nobody answered.

"Who else woulda took it?" Lundy asked. "That's how they are, my pa says. Can't trust 'em as far as you can throw 'em. 'Sides, I ain't the only one what's had somethin' stole since they come to school."

"Someone took my bread last Friday," Wraight Holt said, glaring at John.

"And Mary O'Teale," Lundy added, "she done had her hair ribbon swiped."

Mary nodded. "It's true, Teacher."

"And that rag doll Vella Holt's always carryin' around with her like it's a real baby," Lundy said. "That's gone. All of it since *they*—" he jabbed a finger at John, "come to school."

Christy put her hands on her hips. "Has anyone seen these items taken? Does anyone have any proof that John or his sisters are responsible?"

"That's how thiefs is," Wraight said. "Sneak up on you when you ain't suspectin'."

"I didn't take your things," John said defiantly. "I ain't got no need of 'em."

"All right," Christy said firmly. "Here's what we're going to do. I want everyone to look high and low for these items for the rest of the noon break. Until we can prove what happened to them, there will be no more accusations. And Lundy, I want you to go home for the rest of the day. You know how I feel about fighting."

"But it weren't *my* fault!" Lundy screamed. "It was him—"

"That'll be quite enough, Lundy," David said. "You're lucky we aren't going to expel you."

Lundy sent a poisonous look at John. He spat on the ground. "You'll get yours," he growled. Then he spun on his heel and stomped off, muttering to himself.

— — —

When the fighting was over, Della May went over to her brother and sat beside him. "Bad fightin'," she reported.

"Lundy and John?" Creed asked.

"Yep."

"I figgered as much."

"You think they stole those things like Lundy said?"

"Don't rightly know." Creed leaned back against the tree trunk, sighed, and closed his eyes.

"Creed," Della May said, "Scalawag's bound to turn up. You heard Granny. She ain't hardly never wrong."

Creed didn't answer. That was a bad sign. Creed *always* had something to say.

"I ain't never heard Granny yell the way she did at Pa the other day," Della May said. She picked a piece of grass and chewed on it.

"Nope," was all Creed said.

Della May paused. "You think Pa was the one shot at John?" she asked softly.

"Most likely."

"If someone shot at you," Della May said, "I'd be powerful mad."

Creed opened one eye. "Thank you kindly, Della May." He smiled, but just a little.

"Creed?"

"Hmm?"

"You figger pas are ever wrong about things?"

"Hardly never. That's why they's pas and we's just children."

"Creed?"

"Lordamercy, Della May! Can't you see I'm restin'?"

"You figger Pa'd be right mad if'n I just talked to Hannah now and again?"

For that, Creed opened both eyes. He scratched his head, eyeing her like she'd gone plumb mad. "Talk to 'em to say mean things? Or talk to 'em to say friendly-like things?"

"Friendly-like."

Creed let out a low whistle. "Della May, you'd be a-walkin' on thin ice, girl."

"I've been givin' it some time. And I've come to figger out that Hannah's purty nice. Today she told me she's been lookin' for Scalawag for you every single day since he run off."

Creed gave that some thought. "Every day?"

"Every day. And I believe her, 'cause she likes animals same as you and me. Has a mouse in her pocket, name of Violet."

"Sounds to me like you already done your share o' talkin'."

"Some, maybe."

"Sounds to me like you already done made up your mind, Della May Allen."

"Maybe so."

"Then you don't need me a-tellin' you what to do, do you?"

"No. I s'pose not."

Creed closed his eyes again. Della May got up to leave. She'd only gone a few steps when she heard Creed call, "Della May?"

"Yep?"

"If'n you do decide to do more talkin', tell her thank you kindly about Scalawag."

❧ Twelve ☙

After school that afternoon, Christy hurriedly graded some papers and cleaned the chalkboard. When she was done, she headed straight to Miss Alice's cabin for the weekly Bible study.

Christy had always loved these meetings. Miss Alice would read in her soothing voice while the other women sewed or simply listened. It was a beautiful cabin inside, full of warmth and color. Polished brass candlesticks shone on the mantel. Cherry and pine furniture gleamed in the sunshine. Whenever Christy was there, she felt transported back to her old life in Asheville. It was a place of beauty, of sophistication, a place where the world was full of promise, not despair.

A world, she realized, like the one Doctor MacNeill seemed to be longing for.

Today, however, when Christy entered Miss Alice's cabin, the scene was not at all what she expected. In one corner sat some of the women who came regularly to the meetings. Granny O'Teale and her daughter-in-law, Swannie, were there. Aunt Polly Teague—at ninety-two, the oldest woman in the Cove—was in her favorite rocker. Fairlight Spencer, Christy's close friend, had come, and so had Lety Coburn. Christy was surprised and relieved to see that Mary Allen had come, too.

Still, many faces were missing. One look at the other corner, where Margaret and Louise Washington sat alone, explained why.

How did the word get out so quickly? Christy wondered. But of course she knew the answer. By now she understood that news had a way of traveling fast in Cutter gap—like "greased lightning," as her students liked to say.

"Christy!" Miss Alice exclaimed. "Come, sit down. We were just getting started. You see we have some new faces."

"Margaret, Louise." Christy sat down beside them. "I'm so glad you could come. You, too, Mary."

Mary gave a terse nod, but said nothing.

Christy gazed around her. Most of the women sat on one side. Christy and the Washingtons sat on the other. Miss Alice in the middle, trying to make peace. They were divided into warring camps, separated by hate and misunderstanding. Just like her classroom.

Miss Alice seemed to be reading Christy's mind. "I'll strain my voice, having to read to the east and west side of the cabin. Suppose we all try to move our chairs a little closer?"

No one moved. Margaret studied her Bible. Louise looked as if she were about to cry.

Fairlight cleared her throat. She picked up her chair and moved it next to Louise. "There," Miss Alice said. "That's much better."

Christy looked at her gratefully. Fairlight was a good woman, as warm and gentle as her radiant smile. She would be one ally, at least.

"How was school today, Christy?" Miss Alice asked, clearly hoping to break the icy silence.

Before Christy could answer, Lety Coburn spoke up. "Any more stealin'?" she asked, shooting a look at Margaret. "I hear tell things are disappearin' from that school right and left."

"I don't think it's anything serious, Lety," Christy assured her. "A doll, a hat, some odds and ends. I suspect the children just misplaced them."

"You suspect what you suspect," Lety said, "but I have my own ideas."

Christy sighed. "Is there some reason we can't at least try to get along? On my way here, I passed one of my students playing with Margaret's daughter, Hannah. They were laughing and giggling and having a wonderful time. I think we could all take a lesson from—"

"Whose child was it?" Swannie O'Teale demanded.

"That doesn't matter," Christy said, suddenly realizing she was just making things worse. The last thing she wanted was to get Della May in trouble for having shown some kindness to Hannah. "The point is—"

"Weren't my Mountie or Mary, were it?" Swannie pressed. "I done told those girls to keep their distance."

"Then why are you here?" Margaret spoke up for the first time. "You must have heard we were coming to the Bible study. Everyone seems to know everything in this place."

"I'm here 'cause it's rightfully my place to be here," Swannie jutted her chin. "unlike some."

"If we ain't wanted here," Louise said, leaping from her chair, "then I think we should go, Ma!"

"Louise, please stay," Miss Alice said in a calm, reassuring voice. "Everyone is welcome here in this cabin. This is a place for fellowship and love." She gave Swannie a stern look. "Not intolerance. Christy's right. Let's think about how we can get along. In God's eyes, we are all family, all worthy of His love. I think the key to understanding is to look beyond the surface and see what we all have in common. Before I start today's reading, why don't you tell us a little more about your family, Margaret? Once we get to know one another better, we'll have a better chance at getting along."

Margaret shifted uncomfortably. She clutched her worn Bible to her chest. Christy sent her an encouraging smile.

"Well," Margaret said in a soft voice, "my husband, Curtis and I, we been married all o' sixteen years. Got ourselves four children. Louise here, she's the oldest. She's fifteen. She loves to read, and she's mighty good with the others."

"That's always nice," Fairlight said helpfully. "I don't know what I'd do without Clara and Zady to help out with my young'uns."

Margaret managed a brief smile. "I got two other girls—Hannah, she's eight, and Etta, she's just the baby. Teethin' somethin' fierce, she is."

"Letting her chew on a nice cold rag will help with that," Miss Alice offered.

There was a long pause. Christy thought back to the many other Bible studies she'd been to. They'd been full of lively give-and-take—shared gossip and recipes and tears and laughter. Today, she could almost see the tension in the room.

"And then," Margaret added, eyes trained on the women on the other side of the room, "there's my son, John. He's a good boy—just ten. Somebody shot him the other day. For no reason, 'ceptin' they didn't like the color of his skin."

Her words hung in the air. Louise wiped away a tear.

"He's a fine boy, I'm tellin' you. All my family is," Margaret continued. She opened her Bible and held it up for all to see.

"This here's our family tree. All the names and baptisms wrote down proper-like. These was good people. 'Course, we can't rightly know 'em all—some of our folks were sold off as slaves, never heard of again." Tenderly, she passed the Bible to Christy. "Looky here, Miz Christy. These was good people, all of 'em."

Christy traced her finger over the names on the yellowed page. "I'm sure they were, Margaret."

"See there? William? That be Louise's great-grandpa." Margaret pointed a trembling finger at the name. "He run away from a plantation in Alabama, years before Abraham Lincoln done freed the slaves. Runnin' in leg irons, bleedin' and hungry.

He got hisself to Tennessee, to the mountains. Found a little hidden-away mite of a place. 'No bigger'n a tick's toe,' he used to say. Name o' Cutter Gap. He was fevered and near to dyin'."

Margaret took a deep breath. She looked at Swannie and Mary and the rest of the women. "A good woman from these parts saved Grandpa William. She hid him in a cave, brought him food, and tended to his wounds. She got herself a saw and took them leg irons off her own self. Without her, Grandpa William would have died. And that good woman she also gave him that there Bible and sent him off to freedom, she did."

"Who was this woman, Margaret?" Miss Alice asked.

"She never did give her name. Lots of folks back then used nicknames to protect themselves. Helpin' slaves was a crime. It was right dangerous. And it was mighty brave."

Christy studied the top of the page. There was a simple inscription:

Godspeed, William.
Birdy

"That's why we come here to Cutter Gap," Margaret said, her voice choked. "We knew the stories Grandpa William used to tell. We knew this had to be a place full o' good people. But we was wrong."

She leapt from her chair, pulling the Bible out of Christy's hands.

"Margaret," Christy pleaded, "please stay—"

"No, Miz Christy. Louise and me, we know we ain't wanted here. We'll read our Bible at home. I figure the Lord'll hear us just as clear from there."

❧ Thirteen ❧

I'm sorry the Bible study went so badly," Doctor MacNeill said.

The doctor had stopped by just after the Bible study at Miss Alice's had ended. He was on his way home from delivering a baby.

"It was awful," Christy said as she pulled weeds out of the vegetable garden by the mission house. "Poor Margaret and Louise. The other women were so cold—except for Fairlight, of course."

"Did Mary Allen show up?"

"Yes. But I don't think she said three words the whole time." Christy yanked out a weed, grimacing. "Sometimes I just get so discouraged about this place."

"Sometimes I do, too." The doctor gave a sad smile. "Which is why, I suppose, I'm thinking about asking James for a position."

"Position?" Christy echoed softly.

"Working in his practice in Knoxville. It'd take some time to get my skills up to speed, but I'm sure he'd take me on."

Christy stared at him, dumbfounded. "You mean . . . leave Cutter Gap for good?"

The doctor knelt down. He pulled a weed out of a row of carrots. "I'm not doing much good here, Christy. I have to realize that. I'm fighting a war I can never win."

"How can you say that?" Christy cried. "You just brought a beautiful baby into the world!"

"Babies will keep being born, whether I'm here or not. Miss Alice is more than competent to do what mending or stitching has to be done."

"But—"

The doctor put his finger to Christy's lips. "I know all the arguments. Please. Just let it go, Christy." He stood. "Well, I should get going. I just wanted to remind you that we haven't yet finished a single one of our dance practices. Perhaps later this week—"

"You just expect me to let you off the hook?" Christy demanded. "You tell me you may leave for good, and I'm just supposed to accept it?"

The doctor gave a resigned shrug. "Who knows? Maybe I'll go to Knoxville and get a taste of James's life, and this will look better. I doubt it, but it could happen."

Christy stared at him in shock. He couldn't leave Cutter Gap! The people here needed him.

She needed him.

Just then, two bluejays fluttered into the vegetable patch, ignoring the scarecrow Miss Ida had constructed out of a broom. One nipped at the other, which led to a dreadful screaming match.

"See?" the doctor said. "Even the birds can't seem to get along here."

Suddenly, Christy remembered the signature she'd seen in the Washingtons' Bible. *Birdy*.

Why did that name mean something?

The doctor started for his horse. "Wait," Christy said. "Don't go."

"You can try to talk me out of this later," Doctor MacNeill said wearily. "I was up all night, and I'm too tired to argue with you." He chuckled. "As it is, you usually win."

"No." Christy leapt to her feet, brushing off her dress. "I . . . I just thought of something. Remember that framed needlepoint that Bob broke? The one Granny Allen said she'd made?"

"Yes. Why?"

"Well, there was a bird on the bottom of it. And today, in the Washingtons' Bible . . ."

Yes. That was the connection. That had to be it, Christy thought.

Doctor MacNeill frowned. "I don't follow you."

"That's all right. You will. How tired are you, anyway?"

"Exhausted."

"Then I'll take the reins. Come on."

The doctor crossed his arms over his chest. "And where are we going, exactly?"

"To the Allens'. To do a little detective work."

— — — —

Hannah and Della May skirted the edge of Blackberry Creek. They'd been together all afternoon, ever since school had let out.

For the most part, Della May had been careful to stick to the woods. She liked Hannah just fine, but there was no point in letting Lundy or anybody else see them playing together. That would just make for a heap of trouble. She had a feeling Miz Christy had caught sight of them this afternoon, but that was different. Miz Christy she could trust.

Della May sat on the bank. It was mighty peaceful. You could almost pretend that she and Hannah were just two friends, nothing special. Of course, that wasn't how it really was at all.

"We're gettin' on toward my cabin," she told Hannah. "You'd best be headin' home. If'n my pa caught sight of us, there'd be trouble for sure and certain."

Hannah dipped her toes in the rushing creek. "How come you figure your pa's so dead set against me and my kin?"

"Don't rightly know," Della May said truthfully. "I s'pose 'cause his pa was, and his pa before him."

"Don't seem fair."

"I know. I'm powerful sorry."

Hannah pointed downstream. "I still think we oughta check the trees and such around these parts. Scalawag coulda been headin' for home and got hisself hurt. Messed up with a hound, maybe."

"It's awful nice of you to help me keep lookin' for him. Creed's so sad he's all but given up. Never seen him so down-hearted."

"I had a dog once, got stole. Some white folks took him, drowned him in a well. Tied a rock round his neck." Hannah took a deep breath. "So I know what it's like, losin' a pet and all. We'd have better luck if'n we could look for Scalawag at night. Raccoons is night creatures by nature."

"We'll just have to keep hopin', I guess."

"Della May?" Hannah said softly.

"Yep?"

Hannah's eyes were wet with tears. "I . . . I heard Lundy a-sayin' as how he figured me and John stole Scalawag and skinned him alive. He says we done stole all sorts of things."

"Lundy's a fool. Half the time his head don't know what his mouth is sayin'." Della May patted Hannah on the back. "You don't pay him no never mind. None o' us believes him much either. Creed and me know what's what."

"Thanks, Della May."

"I oughta be thankin' you, for searchin' so hard."

"Let's just look another piece," Hannah said, getting to her feet. "Scalawag could be right around the corner."

"Not too close to my kin, though."

"I promise."

They made their way toward the cabin. It was just visible through the thick stand of trees. Suddenly Hannah jerked to a stop.

"Is that your gray horse?"

"That's Soldier. Pa's horse."

Hannah looked at Della May. Something in her eyes burned like hot coals. "The person who shot John. He was ridin' a gray horse with spots. I saw it through the trees."

Della May didn't know what to say. But she knew she couldn't lie.

"I heard my pa and ma whisperin' about that. I can't tell you one way or t'other what the truth is." She hung her head. "But I'd be lyin' if'n I said I was sure my pa didn't shoot that gun. If'n he did, I 'spect it was just to stir things up. Not to hurt nobody."

"But he did hurt somebody! He hurt John!" Hannah cried.

She spun on her heel and started to run. After a few feet, she stumbled on a tree root.

Della May ran to help her, but Hannah pushed her away. "Go away," she sobbed. "I don't want—"

A horrible scream, coming from the direction of the mill, cut her off.

Della May gulped. "That's my pa! Somethin' awful's happened! I have to go, Hannah. Will you be all right?"

"Go on. Git."

Della May ran as fast her legs would carry her. The screams kept coming, louder, each one more awful than the last.

She was almost to the mill when she saw Creed. "Pa!" he cried. "He passed out again. His arm's caught in the wood gears! We tried and tried, me and Festus and ma and Rob, but we can't budge him. We gotta get help, Della May. He's bleedin' bad."

"You stay here. I'll take Soldier and go for Doctor MacNeill."

Sobbing as she ran, Della May returned to the front yard. She grabbed Soldier's mane and hefted herself onto his back. She was a good rider. Still, she knew it could be a long time before she reached the doctor.

She'd only gone a few feet when she

heard a small voice calling from behind. "Della May! Wait up!"

Della May reined Soldier in. "Hannah?"

"I heard Creed a-yellin' about your pa. Give me a lift up."

"What?"

"We're ridin' to my cabin. It's closer."

"But . . . even after what you said?"

"That's about my pa and yours. This is about you and me. 'Sides, I can't stand to see my best friend a-sobbin'."

Della May shook her head. "You're plumb amazin', Hannah Washington."

"One thing. When we get close, you let me go first. My family ain't goin' to be none too happy to see this horse show up again."

❧ Fourteen ❧

Let me just say this," Doctor MacNeill said as he wrapped a bandage around Bob's arm. "You're a very lucky man that Curtis and John and Margaret came to your aid."

Bob gave a terse nod. The Allen family was gathered by his bedside—all except Granny, who was sitting in her rocker, watching the proceedings. The Washingtons—John, Curtis, Margaret, and Hannah—stood by the door. Louise had stayed home with the baby.

Christy patted John's shoulder. "You saved his life, John, you and your family. I'm so proud of you."

"We come 'cause Hannah begged us to," John muttered. "That's the only reason."

"It must not have been easy, pulling his arm free," Doctor MacNeill said.

"Pa stuck a log in the gears to make 'em

stop," Hannah explained. "Then everybody just yanked and yanked. For a thin man, Mr. Allen, you shore do weigh a heap."

Her remark was met with tense laughter.

"You're going to have to think about getting some help at the mill, Bob." Doctor MacNeill cut another length of bandage. "You can't be losing consciousness that way."

"Boys'll help me. Rob, Festus, Creed. They's old enough."

"But their schooling—" Christy protested.

"Schoolin' ain't nothin', compared to the mill," Bob said.

"Well," Curtis said abruptly, "we'd best be goin'."

"I . . ." Mary hesitated, glancing at Bob. "I want to thank you kindly for helpin'. You bound up his wound right proper, Margaret."

"She certainly did," the doctor said. "Bob would have bled to death without her."

"Had some practice not long ago," Margaret said sharply.

All eyes turned to the bandage on John's arm. Nobody spoke.

"Bob," Granny said sharply, "ain't there somethin' you want to be sayin'?"

Bob winced as Doctor MacNeill tied his bandage into place. "I said all I want to say."

"Ain't surprised," Curtis said. "Wouldn't 'spect no more from the likes of you." He strode over to Bob's bedside. "That horse o' yours. It's just like the one Hannah saw when John was shot. Now, I ain't sayin' for sure you shot my boy, 'cause I don't know. But if I ever catch you near my place with a gun in your hand, you'll be dead before you know what hit you."

The Washingtons filed out the door. Della May ran to the doorway. Nervously, she glanced over her shoulder at her father. "Bye, Hannah," she called softly. "Thank you."

"What's got into you, gal?" Bob shouted as soon as Della May shut the door. "What did I tell you about goin' near them folks?"

"Bob," Christy said, "those people just saved your life."

"I've just about had my fill with your meddlin', Miz Christy," Bob said, falling back against his pillow.

"Bob!" Mary cried. "Miz Christy and the doc are just tryin' to help you."

The doctor closed his bag. "I think we're just about done here, anyway, Mary," he said with barely concealed disgust. "You remember to change that bandage like I showed you."

"I will, Doctor."

"Before we go," Christy said, "we were wondering if we could have a word with you, Granny. It's about the Washingtons."

Granny narrowed her eyes. "I'm afeared I didn't hear you."

Christy smiled. She knew Granny had a way of not hearing when it was convenient.

Christy picked up the needlepoint she'd seen the other day. "This is some fine needlework, Granny. I was wondering why you didn't sign your name to it."

Granny shrugged. "No room, I reckon."

"But you had room to stitch a pretty little bluebird."

Granny yanked the needlepoint out of Christy's hand. "That's from another time, gal. Don't you be a-pesterin' me about such things."

"It's interesting," Christy continued, "because when I was looking at the Washingtons' family Bible, I saw an unusual signature. The woman's name was 'Birdy.'"

Granny studied the needlepoint, head lowered, ignoring Christy.

"Did you have a nickname as a child, Granny?" Christy asked.

"Can't hear you, child."

"'Birdy,' wasn't it?" the doctor said loudly.

"Pshaw." Granny waved him away. "Talkin' nonsense, the both of you. Crazy as March hares."

"I know it was Birdy," the doctor continued, "because I can remember my own grandma saying it. When Christy mentioned it today, it all came back to me."

"You're not sayin' that Granny is the

woman . . ." Mary gasped. "The woman Mary Washington was speakin' of at Bible study?"

"What in tarnation are you fools cacklin' about?" Bob demanded from his bed.

"Tell him, Granny," Christy urged gently. "Tell him what that young woman nicknamed Birdy did."

Granny just stared at the needlepoint in her lap, running her gnarled fingers over the needlework.

"Would somebody please tell me what all this nonsense is about?" Bob cried.

"Miz Christy's sayin' that Granny helped save one of the Washingtons' kin, Bob," Mary said. She was staring at Granny with a bewildered look. "A . . . a slave. Before the war. A long time ago."

"Long time," Granny whispered.

"It's true, isn't it, Granny?" Christy said.

Granny looked up at Christy. Her eyes were damp. She shook her head slightly.

"You can't squeeze milk out of a rock, Miz Christy," Bob said defiantly. "And you can't make what ain't true a fact. Why, Granny's the one who was all in a tizzy when she heard the Washingtons were movin' in! You got your stories all backward. But then," he added bitterly, "you got a lot o' things backward lately."

Doctor MacNeill knelt beside Granny. He took her hand and held it gently. "Granny," he said softly, "my own granny often spoke of you with such respect. She used to say you were tough as a laurel burl and braver than any man. Now, at last, I think I understand what she meant. I know you were afraid to admit it before. But now's the time. Tell them, Granny. Tell them what you did. Maybe it will help heal the wounds in this place. Maybe it's not too late to change things."

Della May put her arm around her great-grandmother's frail back. "Is it true, Granny? Is it true what the doctor is sayin'?"

Granny gave a resigned, faraway smile. "I can't hear you, child," she whispered.

❧ Fifteen ❧

That evening, Christy wrote in her diary before going to bed, hoping to rid herself of the heavy feeling in her heart. But she wondered if anything could really ease the pain.

Where are the answers when I need them? So much seems to be going wrong, and nothing I do helps. Doctor MacNeill says he's thinking of leaving the Cove for good. Granny Allen refuses to acknowledge her courageous act of so long ago. And I can't seem to get through to anyone.

Every day at school the hatred toward the Washingtons simmers. The accusations of stealing get more intense, but when I try to soothe my students, they ask me for an explanation. Why have things been disappearing from school? Why did it start right around the time John and Louise and Hannah arrived?

*I know there must be an explanation. They're
such good children. But for the life of me, I can't
figure out what it is.*

*Today, after we left the Allens' cabin, Neil
told me that some people will never change. That
there will always be feuding and racism and hatred
in people—especially the people of Cutter Gap.*

*Never have I seen him so cynical. So dark.
Or so unhappy.*

*I told him that there is goodness in people. I
told him how Fairlight had moved her chair at the
Bible study. I told him how I'd seen Della May
and Hannah playing together, despite all the risks.*

*I told him we just had to wait and work and
pray.*

And all he did was laugh.

Christy put her diary away. There was
nothing more to say or do. Except, perhaps,
to cry. And pray.

〜 〜 〜

Late that night, Christy awoke suddenly,
feeling anxious. She sat up, letting her eyes
adjust to the darkness. Something was wrong.
Was that smoke she smelled?

She ran to the open window. The smell of
burning wood was in the air. Far up on
Kildeer Mountain, red flames flickered against
the night sky.

Christy's heart leapt into her throat. That was where Doctor MacNeill lived! It could be his cabin burning, or the Allens', or . . .

No.

Please, God, Christy silently prayed, *don't let it be the Washingtons' cabin. Let it be a forest fire, a campfire out of control, a woodpile . . .*

She threw on a dress and her shoes and raced down the stairs, just as David burst through the front door. Miss Ida was already up, dressed in her nightgown and robe.

"Looks like Kildeer," David said breathlessly. "I'm taking Prince up."

"I'm coming, too," Christy said. "Let me ride with you."

"Could it be a forest fire?" Miss Ida asked.

"Woods are pretty damp. No lightning," David replied. "But I suppose it could be."

"Do you think it's the Washingtons' place?" Miss Ida asked.

"I fear it is," Christy replied, "but I'm praying it isn't."

David urged Prince on as fast as he dared, but in the dark, every tree root and hole in the mountain path was treacherous. The closer they got to the fire, the larger it seemed to grow.

Red-gold flames licked at the stars. The air

grew acrid with the smell of burning wood. In the stillness of the night woods, the sound of the crackling fire grew ominous. Before long, they could hear the sound of desperate shouts.

Soon it was clear that the fire was located at the Washingtons'. "The flames are going higher," David said grimly, "but they're not spreading, the way they would with a forest fire. It must be their cabin."

"We should have kept this from happening," Christy muttered. "Surely there was something we could have done."

David glanced over his shoulder. His face was barely visible in the moonlight. "We tried, Christy."

"Not hard enough. And that makes me feel almost as guilty as the people who did this."

For the rest of the ride, neither spoke. There was nothing more to say. It was too late for words.

Just let them be all right, Christy prayed. *They can build another cabin. Just let the family be all right.*

❧ Sixteen ☙

By the time they reached the clearing where the Washingtons' cabin was located, the fire had quieted. It was more smoke than flame, but the damage was already done.

Doctor MacNeill was there, tossing buckets of dirt on the dying embers. His face and hands were darkened by soot. Curtis and John were still fighting the fire, too. They'd saved a few things—a chair, an iron pot, a photograph. But the cabin itself was nothing but charred logs, glowing an eerie red in the night. Christy ran to the spot where Margaret and the girls stood huddled together. Margaret was clutching their worn Bible.

"Margaret, I'm so sorry," Christy said, hugging the trembling woman. "Are you all right? Was anyone hurt?"

"We're fine. Curtis, he got some burns on his

hands. Doc, too." She let out a soft sob. "The children's all right. That's all that matters."

Doctor MacNeill came over. His brow was damp with perspiration. "Neil," Christy asked, "are you hurt?"

"A few burns. Nothing much." He shook his head at the dying embers where the little cabin had stood. "Do you see now why I want to leave this place? Tell me this, Christy. Can you look at this and still tell me there's good in the people of Cutter Gap?"

"You can't blame everyone, Doctor," David said. "This isn't the work of the whole Cove."

"No," the doctor said bitterly. "It's the work of Bob Allen. But there's plenty more where he came from."

Hannah tugged on the doctor's shirt. "Truth to tell, Doctor MacNeill," she said in a teary voice, "it weren't Bob."

"Hannah?" Margaret asked. "Did you see who done this, child?"

"I heard a noise, Ma, right before it started. Saw three men outa the window. All of 'em on horses, dark ones. Not gray like Bob's."

"She's right. With Bob's arm in such sorry shape, he'd be in no condition to ride," the doctor said wearily. "I shouldn't have assumed as much. But it doesn't help to hear there are others like him out there. Not that it's exactly a surprise."

Curtis came over, wiping his face with the

back of his arm. "Well, I guess they're gettin' their way," he said grimly. "I can fight words, maybe even bullets. But I can't fight fire."

"Yes, you can, Bob," Christy said firmly. "You fight fire with fire. When someone burns down your house, you build it up again. That way you don't let them win."

"It's too late for that, Miz Christy. I gotta think o' my children."

"Pa?" Hannah said softly. "What if we move on and they just burn us down all over again?"

"What if we stay," Curtis said, "and they do it again right here?" He knelt beside Hannah and held her close. "Sweetie, ol' Grandpa William was wrong about Cutter Gap. He said he felt closer to God here. But the truth is, I ain't never felt Him further away."

❦ ❦ ❦

"Granny?" Della May said after school the next day. "I got me a question for you." She sat next to her great-grandmother on the dusty wooden porch outside the Allens' cabin.

"What is it, girl?"

Della May checked over her shoulder to be sure her pa and ma weren't around. "Where's Pa?" she asked.

"Out to the mill, the old coot. He ain't got a lick o' sense. His arm bandaged up and his head a-swimmin'."

"Well, it's like this. You know how the Washingtons' cabin done got burned down last night?"

"Could see those flames for miles."

"Well, Hannah weren't in school today. Her brother and sister, neither."

Granny looked up from her knitting. Her old fingers always moved very slowly, but now they stopped.

"Teacher said they was stayin' at the mission house. Said they might be a-movin' on soon, and it were all our faults for not bein' more friendly."

"Miz Christy's full of notions," Granny said softly.

"Granny, I have a confession to make. It's a-burning up my soul somethin' fierce."

"Speak your mind, then."

Della May took a deep breath. "Hannah Washington . . . well, she's the best friend I ever had, 'sides Creed. I don't want her to go, Granny. Is that wrong?"

Very slowly, Granny set her knitting aside. She reached for Della May's hand and grasped it tightly. "You're a fine girl, Della May. And it's a fine thing to have a friend, no matter what color she is."

"Is it true, Granny?" Della May asked. "What Miz Christy said about you savin' that slave way back when?"

Granny rocked back and forth. "What if it was? What would you think o' your ol' granny then?"

Della May thought for a while. "I know how hard it's been to be Hannah's friend. Us always dodgin' from people and sneakin' in the woods and all. So I guess if'n you really *was* Birdy, I'd have to say I'd be powerful proud. Considerin' how brave she musta been."

For a long time, Granny didn't reply. She had thinking spells like that a lot, and Della May knew better than to bother her. She sat quietly on the porch by her great-grandmother, waiting and wondering and feeling sad. She felt like someone had torn a hole right out of her middle. She felt empty and smaller and very lonely.

"Child," Granny said suddenly. "I want you to go fetch your pa."

"He don't like it when I trouble him at the mill, Granny. What if he asks how come?"

Granny took a long breath. "Just tell him Birdy wants to see him."

ஃ Seventeen ஃ

We sure can't thank you enough for givin' us a roof over our heads," Curtis said in the mission house dining room the next morning. The Washingtons had just finished breakfast, along with Christy, Miss Ida, and Ruby Mae. Miss Alice, Doctor MacNeill, and David were there, too.

"We were glad to help," Christy replied. "I just wish you would stay a little longer. There's plenty of room. Why do you have to leave so soon?"

"I got to find me some work as soon as possible, Miz Christy," Curtis replied. "There'll be somethin' in Knoxville. It's a big city."

"So Doctor MacNeill tells me," Christy said, sending a meaningful look at the doctor.

"Maybe we'll run into each other, Doctor," Curtis said. "If'n you decide to move on, too."

"I certainly wish we could convince you and the doctor to stay put," said Miss Alice.

"So it's true, Doctor?" David asked. "You're really leaving Cutter Gap?"

"I'm seriously considering the possibility. It feels like it's time to make a change." The doctor gave a wry grin. "Was that a note of hope I heard in your voice, Reverend?"

David grinned. "Not at all. I'll certainly miss you . . . professionally, anyway. This Cove needs a good doctor. Miss Alice has too much to take care of as it is."

"We'll get by," Miss Alice said. She sipped at her tea, then gave the doctor a sad smile. "Neil needs to do what's best for him."

"We've got plenty of work to be done around the mission, Curtis," David said. "You could stay for a while, work off your room and board that way."

"That wouldn't really solve the problem, now, would it?" Curtis shoved back his chair. "Come on, children. We've got a long walk ahead of us, if'n we want to make El Pano today."

"We're hopin' to leave before school gets started," Margaret whispered to Christy. "It'll be easier on the children that way."

On the porch, Christy knelt down beside Hannah. "I want you to promise to write me, Hannah," she said, "and let me know how you and John and Louise are doing."

"Miz Christy," Hannah said, her eyes full of tears, "would you tell Della May I said goodbye?"

"Of course."

"And would you tell Creed I'm a-keepin' my fingers crossed that Scalawag turns up?"

"Of course I—" Christy paused, shading her eyes from the morning sun. Who was that, heading down the path to the mission house?

"I have a better idea, Hannah," Christy said. "Why don't you tell them yourself?"

"Why, I'll be," Hannah cried. "It's all them Allens!"

"Even Granny," the doctor said.

"Probably come here to gloat," John muttered. "See us run out, just the way they wanted."

"Let's get goin'," Curtis said gravely. "Ain't no need for us to put up with them no longer."

But Della May was already running up the steps of the mission house, ahead of the others. "Hannah!" she cried. "Are you a-leavin' already?"

Hannah nodded. "We're movin' on to the city."

"But you *can't* go, you just can't! Leastways, not till Pa and Granny says their piece." She tugged on Curtis's sleeve. "Please, Mr. Washington. Please hear them out."

"We heard all we needed to hear from your pa and his shotgun," John snapped.

"But my granny come all this way, with her rheumatis' and all," Della May protested.

Christy put her hand on Curtis's arm. "Maybe you should hear what they have to say, Curtis."

"Please, Curtis," Margaret said softly. "We been through this much. A few more words can't hurt us."

Hobbling slowly, clutching at Mary's arm, Granny Allen made her way to the house. Bob hung behind, hands in his pockets. The other Allen children followed.

"We come to talk," Granny announced when they'd reached the porch.

"Say what you got to say," Curtis said sharply. "We need to be movin' on."

Granny motioned to Bob. "Go on, then. Be a man and speak your mind."

Bob cleared his throat. "I been doin' some thinkin'," he said, choosing each word with care. "Well, mostly, Granny's been doin' some talkin'." He looked up at Curtis. "Granny's the one what saved your grandpa, turns out."

Margaret gasped. *"You? You're* Birdy?"

"That was my growin'-up name," Granny said. "Used it with William to protect myself." She shook her head. "Did a lot o' protectin' after that. Worryin' if'n anyone found out about what I done, what might happen. Never told a soul, 'ceptin' one friend."

"But why?" Louise asked softly.

"People woulda turned agin me. Maybe even strung me up to die. Things are better some now . . . but not much. I was afraid, child." Her lower lip trembled. "But Della May made me think maybe what I done weren't so awful after all. Maybe it was even a good thing. How many of us get the chance to save a man's life?"

"My granny's a good woman," Bob said. "Stubborn as a mad mule, but good. So I've been startin' to think maybe I might be wrong about some things."

"What he means is, I told this ornery, cantankerous old cuss that he better think twice about the way he was treatin' William Washington's kinfolk." Granny winked. "'Cause William was a friend of mine, and I aim to do right by him."

"Granny and Ma done yelled at Pa from sunup to sundown," Della May confided in a loud whisper to Hannah.

Bob rolled his eyes. "That's enough outa you, young'un."

Curtis stepped down to Granny and took her hand. "It's an honor to meet you, Ma'am. On behalf of all my kin, I want to thank you for what you done. None of us would be here without you." He sighed. "But that's all in the past. We still got to be movin' on."

"Not so fast, young man!" Granny cried. "My Bob ain't done with his speechifyin'. *Are* you, Bob?"

Bob kicked at the ground with his toe. "The thing is . . ." he cleared his throat, "the thing of it is, seems I need some help at the mill. I get these spells, and . . . well, if'n you'd be willin' to work, my boys and I could maybe help you build yourself a new cabin." He shrugged. "If'n you wanted."

"We're already set on leavin'," Curtis said tersely. "Why stay in a place where people burn your cabin to the ground?"

"There's good people, too, Pa," Hannah said. "Della May and Creed, they's good as they come. And Miz Christy and the preacher and Doctor MacNeill. And Granny." She smiled shyly at Granny Allen. "You said yourself Grandpa William woulda liked us settlin' here."

Curtis shook his head. "I just don't think . . ."

"My, but you're the spittin' image of William!" Granny exclaimed. "Never could argue him outa anything. I was afeared he couldn't make it north, but oh, he was set in his ways somethin' fierce. 'Birdy,' he said, 'scares me awful to try. But it scares me worse not to.'"

Curtis smiled, just a little. "He was a brave man, that Grandpa William."

"So are you, Pa," Hannah whispered. "You ain't a-scared o' tryin'."

For a long time, Curtis stared off at the mountaintops, reaching up to the morning sky. At last, he walked over to Bob. They faced each other, eye to eye.

"We'll try it for a month," Curtis said. He held out his hand.

Bob stared at it, hesitating. "I ain't never shook hands with one of your kind," he admitted. He gave a resigned sigh. "But I s'pose I ain't a-scared o' tryin', either."

Slowly, reluctantly, the two men grasped hands.

❧ ❧ ❧

Before the Allens left, Granny motioned Christy and the doctor aside. "I want to thank the two of you," she said. "I was afraid to admit what I done. But that's who I am, and I s'pose, all things considered, I'm glad of it."

"I wonder, Granny," the doctor said, "who was it you told about William? My grandmother always looked up to you so. I wondered if . . ."

"Factually speakin', I did confide in your granny, Doc. I needed someone to fetch me a saw so's I could remove William's leg irons. I was desperate, and I took Helen aside and told her the whole truth."

"And she helped you?" Christy asked.

"Well, not quite." Granny hesitated. "She said she was afraid to help me. But on the other hand, she never breathed a word of my secret to anyone else. And that was a kind of help, don't you see?"

"So she was afraid," the doctor said, sounding a little disappointed.

"Oh, we all get afraid from time to time, Doctor MacNeill." Granny patted his arm gently. "She was a fine woman, your granny. You know how it is. We do what we can."

The doctor smiled sadly. "Some of us do, anyway."

✂ Eighteen ✂

A week later, Christy was sitting with the children during the noon break when she saw Doctor MacNeill riding up.

He dismounted and joined her on the lawn.

"I haven't heard from you in several days," she said. "I was starting to worry."

"I'm sorry. I've been preoccupied. I've been thinking, mostly . . . working some. The Washingtons' cabin's coming along nicely."

"It's nice of you to help out."

"It's the least I can do." The doctor lay back on the lawn, staring up at the sky. "I have to compensate for my dear departed grandmother."

"Not everyone can be as brave as Granny Allen was," Christy said. "I'm not sure I'd have that kind of courage."

The doctor sat up and pulled an envelope out of his breast pocket. "Has Ben Pentland been by yet with the mail?"

"No. But he's due today. Would you like me to give that to him?"

"Thanks." The doctor passed her the envelope. Christy slipped it into a book.

"Aren't you at least going to read the address?"

"Of course not. That's your private concern."

"It's to James," the doctor said.

Christy felt her heart plummet. "Is it about the job?"

"Yes. I felt it was time."

"I understand." Christy looked away to hide the tears threatening to spill down her cheeks. "I'm awfully disappointed, Neil . . ."

"I'm sorry. I know you had your heart set on waltzing at the wedding. Not to mention showing off your Italian."

Christy blinked. She looked at the doctor, eyes narrowed. "I don't think I heard you right . . ."

"Well, if I'm not going to take the job in Knoxville, I figured there was no point in going all the way there just to show you off. After all, you're a beautiful woman, Christy. Who knows what might happen if I let all those eligible young doctors get a glimpse of you?"

"You're not . . . you're not leaving us?"

Christy threw her arms around the doctor's neck and kissed him.

The children broke into wild applause, laughing and pointing. Quickly Christy pulled away, her cheeks ablaze.

"My, my," the doctor said. "I had no idea I was in danger of being so sorely missed."

"I'm just glad for the Cove," Christy said demurely. "That's all."

"Well, I very much enjoyed kissing you on behalf of the Cove," the doctor replied.

"But why did you change your mind?" Christy asked, smiling in spite of herself.

"Oh, a lot of things, I suppose. Seeing the Washingtons decide to stay. Whatever hardships I have, it's nothing compared to what they're up against. And hearing about my grandmother, Helen. I felt she'd let Cutter Gap down, just a little, that day Granny Allen asked for her help. I sort of feel like I need to make it up to this place. It's crazy, I know."

"Not at all."

The doctor leapt to his feet. "And then there was you."

"Me?"

He nodded. "See, I'm aiming to enter next year's state waltzing championship. And I know just the girl I want as a partner."

Christy stood, smiling. "Really? Anyone I know?"

"She speaks only one language. Her father

isn't a rich industrialist. And she's not much of a dancer, either."

"What do you see in her, I wonder?"

The doctor swept Christy into his arms, and they began to waltz, spinning around and around. The children watched, mesmerized.

"It's hard to say why I'm so fond of her," he said. "Could be because she loves these mountains as much as I do."

━ ━ ━

When the break was over, Christy herded the last of the straggling children into the school. They'd been teasing her about her kiss and her dance with the doctor for an hour now. It was going to be a long afternoon. But at least that would make for a change from the tension still hovering in the air around the Washington children.

It wasn't enough, she knew, for Bob Allen to hire Curtis. It wasn't enough that the Washingtons' cabin was being rebuilt. The older boys still tormented John and Louise and Hannah whenever they could. Ugly words were still being whispered. Even Hannah and Della May still hid their friendship.

Christy paused on the steps. Was everyone inside? She caught sight of Della May and Hannah, far off at the edge of the woods. "Girls!" she called. "Hurry up! No more dawdling!"

"Teacher!" Della May cried. She pointed to an old oak tree. "Come see! Bring everyone and come see, now!"

Christy frowned. The girls were taking an awful risk being seen together this way.

"It's important, Miz Christy!" Della May called. "I promise!"

Christy shook her head. Well, she wasn't eager to face a spelling lesson, either. After the doctor's good news, she almost felt like playing hooky herself. "All right, then," she called back, "but this had better be good, girls."

She poked her head in the schoolroom door. "Children," she called, "follow me."

Christy lead the way toward the old oak, trailed by her eager students. "Where are we goin', Teacher?" Little Burl asked.

"Actually, I have no idea, Little Burl," Christy confessed.

Della May and Hannah were standing side-by-side next to the tree. There was a large hollow under the lowest branch, just about even with the girls' heads.

"Well," Christy announced, "we're all here."

"We got somethin' to show y'all," Della May announced. She put her arm around Hannah's shoulder.

"What are you doin' with the likes o' her?"

Lundy demanded of Della May. "Your hand'll wither up and fall off now, sure as anything."

"Hush, Lundy," Della May said firmly. "First off, Creed gets to look."

The girls stepped aside and motioned for Creed. He peered inside the dark hole and gasped, hand to his mouth.

"Shh," Hannah said, grinning. "Don't tell!"

"It was all Hannah's doin', Creed," Della May said. "She done found the hole."

"Now for Miz Christy," Della May said.

Christy peered inside the hole. There, to her amazement, were a mother raccoon and four tiny babies.

"Scalawag?" Christy whispered.

"Sure as shootin'," Creed said.

"But I thought he was a boy."

"Guess he had other ideas," Creed said.

"Did you see the nest?" Hannah asked.

Christy looked again. The raccoons were nestled inside an old felt hat. It was lined with a hair ribbon, a rag doll, a plaid shirt, and a piece of chalk, among other things.

"He always was a bit of a thief," Creed admitted. "Can't help hisself. Or herself, I guess I should say."

"Class," Christy said, "Hannah and Della May have something I think you'll be very interested in seeing. It seems we've found Scalawag. And in doing so, we've also located our classroom thief. I think we all owe the Washingtons a very big apology."

Instantly, the children crowded around the hole, jockeying for position.

"My hat!" Lundy cried. "Why, you furry little crook, you!"

"My dolly!" Vella exclaimed. "The babies are sleepin' with my dolly!"

John and Louise watched silently, standing far off to one side. No one apologized. No one even acknowledged that they were there.

Christy heard laughter and turned. Behind her, heading up the school steps, were Hannah and Della May. They were holding hands and giggling, as if they didn't have a care in the world.

It wasn't enough, Christy knew. Not at all.

But at least it was a start.

About the Author

Catherine Marshall

With *Christy*, Catherine Marshall LeSourd (1914–1983) created one of the world's most widely read and best-loved classics. Published in 1967, the book spent 39 weeks on the New York Times bestseller list. With an estimated 30 million Americans having read it, *Christy* is now approaching its 90th printing and has sold more than eight million copies. Although a novel, *Christy* is in fact a thinly-veiled biography of Catherine's mother, Leonora Wood.

Catherine Marshall LeSourd also authored *A Man Called Peter*, which has sold more than four million copies. It is an American bestseller, portraying the love between a dynamic man and his God, and the tender, romantic love between a man and the girl he married. *Julie* is a powerful, sweeping novel of love and adventure, courage and commitment, tragedy and triumph, in a Pennsylvania town during the Great Depression. Catherine also authored many other devotional books of encouragement.

THE CHRISTY® FICTION SERIES

You'll want to read them all!

Based upon Catherine Marshall's international bestseller *Christy®*, this new series contains expanded adventures filled with romance, intrigue, and excitement.

#1—The Bridge to Cutter Gap
Nineteen-year-old Christy leaves her family to teach at a mission school in the Great Smoky Mountains. On the other side of an icy bridge lie excitement, adventure, and maybe even the man of her dreams . . . but can she survive a life-and-death struggle when she falls into the rushing waters below? (ISBN 0-8499-3686-1)

#2—Silent Superstitions
Christy's students are suddenly afraid to come to school. Is what Granny O'Teale says true? Is their teacher cursed? Will the children's fears and the adults' superstitions force Christy to abandon her dreams and return to North Carolina? (ISBN 0-8499-3687-X)

#3—The Angry Intruder
Someone wants Christy to leave Cutter Gap, and they'll stop at nothing. Mysterious pranks soon turn dangerous. Could a student be the culprit? When Christy confronts the late-night intruder, will it be a face she knows? (ISBN 0-8499-3688-8)

#4—Midnight Rescue
The mission's black stallion, Prince, has vanished, and so has Christy's student Ruby Mae. Christy must brave the guns of angry moonshiners to bring them home. Will her faith in God see her through her darkest night? (ISBN 0-8499-3689-6)

#5—The Proposal
Christy should be thrilled when David Grantland, the handsome minister, proposes marriage, but her feelings of excitement are mixed with confusion and uncertainty. Several untimely interruptions delay her answer to David's proposal. Then a terrible riding accident and blindness threaten all of Christy's dreams for the future. (ISBN 0-8499-3918-6)

#6—Christy's Choice
When Christy is offered a chance to teach in her hometown, she faces a difficult decision. Will her train ride back to Cutter Gap be a journey home or a last farewell? In a moment of terror and danger, Christy must decide where her future lies. (ISBN 0-8499-3919-4)

#7—The Princess Club
When Ruby Mae, Bessie, and Clara discover gold at Cutter Gap, they form an exclusive organization, "The Princess Club." Christy watches in dismay as her classroom—and her community—are torn apart by greed, envy, and an understanding of what true wealth really means. (ISBN 0-8499-3958-5)

#8—Family Secrets
Bob Allen and many of the residents of Cutter Gap are upset when a black family, the Washingtons, moves in near the Allens' property. When a series of threatening incidents befall the Washingtons, Christy steps in to help. But it's a clue in the Washingtons' family Bible that may hold the real key to peace and acceptance. (ISBN 0-8499-3959-3)